GW00458185

7 ↗3

SURREY
COUNTY COUNCIL

Overdue items may incur charges
as published in the current
Schedule of Charges.

L21

ISBN: 9798544729518

PublishNation
www.publishnation.co.uk

1960

'Bitch! Oh, what a bitch!'

Our village was in a whirl about a famous actress coming to our World War 2 commemoration but, personally, I was furious.

It was May 1960, 20 years since Millside was bombed in the run up to the Blitz and, as part of the national commemoration of the war, we were having our own ceremony. We thought it would be a rather low-key affair but suddenly out of the blue it was announced that none other than Suzie Bell would be coming and laying a stone on Ben's burial place. Yes, THAT Suzie Bell, the star of many B movies, mostly war-set weepies, very popular with the matinee audiences of housewives and pensioners.

You may think that she had every right to be there and that would be true, but fact is that she never bothered with Ben and, to me, she was just doing a publicity stunt to revive a somewhat flagging career. And, of course, all the circus was there: local press, popular rags, even our local TV station, so Ben was getting all the attention he never had. So much so that nobody had a thought to spare for me even if I had been a key figure in the whole story, besides having been away from the village for many years.

But I am running ahead, as usual. My name is Annie and on that day I had returned to Millside for the event and a sort of personal pilgrimage. I had revisited my old haunts, walked down the High Street where our shop used to be, and knocked on Mrs. Bassett's door.

Dear Mrs. Bassett! She looked older of course, but her kind smile was still there. I had spent a few weeks at her place after the bombing and I asked her to let me into my old room for a while. She did so and, with the excuse of making me a cuppa, tactfully went downstairs and left me by myself. The room had not changed much, except for new curtains and a lick of paint on the walls, but, just as I hoped, the furniture was still the same. So, I went to the old wardrobe that dominated the room and pulled out the heavy bottom drawer. At the back there was a small recess and in it I found what I was looking for: my old diary, scorched, blotched by dampness, with pages missing, but still there, a witness of the events of that fateful year. As I began to read it everything came back, the feelings, the faces, the fear.

Mon 18 Dec 1939

16 TODAY

Dad got me this diary for my 16th birthday. It's a beautiful notebook with a blue cover. He says that as he's bound to go to war I should keep a record of my life so he can catch up with me when he comes back. I told him, rather grandly, that grown up girls don't show their personal diaries to their Dads but he replied that we are old pals and we have no secrets from one another. Well, I think he somewhat deludes himself but it's true that I get on with him much better than with Mum and that working together in the shop makes us closer. We share jokes, sometimes at the expense of our most difficult customers, like stuck up Mr. Cribbles, with his serious self-important air and his silly moustache that bears a passing resemblance to Hitler's.

Sometimes I wish I could get on with Mum in the same way, but it doesn't work. Mum and I are too different and anyway she seems to be more interested in my brother Robert than in me. He is still her "baby" even if he is 13 and she is very proud of him and his "academic achievements" as she puts it. Well, if I had gone to a posh school like him, I might have achieved something as well. ...me jealous? Nooo!

AND TODAY IS MY BIRTHDAY!!!

Was I jealous then? No, I don't think so. Anyway, I don't know whether a posh school would have suited me, as I am a rather matter-of-fact person. And, thinking of it, that is why my mother and I didn't see eye to eye on most matters. Fact is that Mother had social aspirations that I didn't share in the least. She faithfully attended every meeting of the Parish Council, now re-named the War Committee, which she saw as occasions to rub shoulders with the most influential people in our rather restricted "society". It never occurred to her that she was seen rather as a hanger on than as a fully-fledged member of that select group and that when tasks were organised and allocated, she was regularly landed with the most menial and least pleasant ones. She was also part of the WAAF, the Women's Auxiliary Air Force, and carried out her duties with conscience, if not always with competence.

I sometimes think that she saw Robert's schooling as a way to go up in our world through him. She, a small-town miss, had met my father at a country fête and had fallen in love with him. Being a mere shopkeeper's wife wasn't enough for her and that is why I was made to help Dad as soon as I left school while she withdrew almost completely from the day-to-day running of the business. Not that she had contributed much before. In those days before modern appliances appeared in British homes, being a housewife was almost a full-time job. And that, Mum did very well. After all it's not easy to run a household, raise two children, and still manage to look quite "classy". She was a pretty blonde in her late thirties who always tried to dress her best. Myself, at that stage, I was still a bit of a tomboy and dressing well wasn't my main concern. But you mustn't think I was a scruff. I too was a pretty blonde starting to show the right curves in the right places and in addition I had an infectious smile which people found attractive and a light scattering of freckles.

Weds 20 Dec

Call this Christmas? Thanks to the blackout for the first time, there are no lights, let alone Christmas lights, in the High Street. And of course no children knocking at the door singing carols and holding their lanterns. I cannot believe I would miss them and their noise!!!

well, I do but I certainly don't miss Grace Cummings' smug, saintly face as she leads the little choir.

And that wasn't the only sound missing, church bells didn't ring anymore. Instead, we got sirens whose shrieking sound announced an impending air raid. That first Christmas at war was particularly felt by my generation. Our parents had been through that experience in the Great War but for us kids it brought an unfamiliar sense of terror and upheaval, but also a feeling of excitement and adventure. Not even the darkness of that winter, made worse by the blackout and by cowering in the shelters, could take that feeling away. After the alarm ended we would go back to the High Street and resume our normal life, but still feeling the thrill of the avoided danger.

Oh yes, the High Street. With or without lighting, it was nothing special. A few shops including ours, Corbett's Hardware Supplies, the pub at one end and the school at the other. And of course the post office, run by widow Fletcher and the church with the vicarage. This was the home of Vicar Horace Cummings, his wife Amelia and their children Grace and Philip.

Grace and I were the same age, had been sitting in the same classroom since year 1 and totally disliked one another. My mother was keen on me being Grace's friend and tried to push me in her way, in an attempt to get in the good graces of Grace's mother. Anyway, it didn't work. Grace didn't miss any chance to show off her social superiority and would wrinkle her little nose at me.

'You smell of paint.' she would say, stuck-up little cow that she was! I on my part would go out of my way to pay her back and made sure to shake my pen when she was close by, in order to deposit large blots of ink on her immaculate white blouse.

She was always dressed very properly, if dully. She had lovely dark brown hair always well plaited and a pretty face somewhat spoiled by a rather snooty expression. In fact, what I really disliked about her was her "holier than thou" attitude. She was, or appeared to be, pious, virtuous, studious and a bore.

But back to the village now. Millside didn't have any distinguishing features itself, except for the ancient watermill of its name. However, the neighbouring area could boast Albany Court, the posh school where Robert was a day boarder, and the even posher Manor House.

My mother would have given anything to become part of the privileged few allowed to enter its pearly gates, but her contacts with them stopped at the newly named War Committee. Its role now included fire-watching, blackout monitoring and air defence warnings. It also included the billeting of evacuees. In that period thousands of children were being evacuated – that is, taken from their families in places likely to be bombed, like London, and moved to the safety of the countryside. Rural communities were expected to host the brats and keep them out of harm's way in exchange for a small sum and the feeling of helping to "Save the Future of Our Country" as the slogan went.

Fri 22 Dec

AARGH!!!!

As if all that is going on was not enough, today we had another "surprise". Auntie Betty had decided to evacuate herself on us (sounds rude, doesn't it?) Anyway, the very same Auntie Betty that Robert in a bout of creativity that nearly justifies his school fees has re-named Batty Betty, adding the immortal lines:

Batty Betty is so petty

I would throw her off the jetty

Cut her up into confetti

To get rid of Batty Betty

Good eh?

She arrived unannounced and uninvited and, of course, with several bags, her gas mask and her horrible little mutt Doug, and here is my poetic offering:

Doug, the horrible pug with an ugly mug

Not much, I admit it but then I left school at 14. And Doug is not a pug but a little Yorkshire terrier forever yapping and with a nasty nipping habit. The worse of it is that it was decided that Auntie Betty and naturally Doug should share my bedroom. Anyway in a moment of inspiration (or *rather desperation) I nobly offered to let her have my room and to move in the spare room in the basement. It is a bit dark and smells weird but not half as much as Doug.*

As I read that, the scene came alive in my mind. I could see Auntie Betty standing there in frozen surprise at my generous offer and yet still managing to look disapproving. The problem with her was that she disapproved of nearly everything and everybody, a sour-looking spinster with an even sourer temper. She was my mother's sister, about 10 years older than Mum and, according to her, she had sacrificed herself for the good of the family. She had never married, Betty maintained, to help look after her younger siblings, discounting the obvious fact that it would have been VERY difficult to find somebody foolish enough to marry her. Whatever the truth of the matter, she had a definite hold over my mother, sometimes much to my father's annoyance.

Age hadn't improved either her nature or her looks. Auntie Betty talked constantly in a high-pitched voice and gave her view on everything and anything. She wore a sickly Parma Violets perfume which, she announced, was very refined. She favoured pastel-coloured blouses that stretched across her ample bosom and thick black skirts hairy from the dog, together with wrinkly stockings and clumpy shoes. Her mousy hair was nightly tortured by rollers but unfortunately to little effect and the rouge she applied liberally to her cheeks only made the rest of her face look pasty.

Mon 25 Dec

Christmas Day

We look so much towards Christmas, but when it comes it is sometimes a bit of a let-down and this year it was particularly so. I know, we are at war and all, so we accept the fact that we won't get many presents and that the Christmas cheer is not so cheerful after all. Anyway, what nearly did it for us was the NEFARIOUS (good word eh? I borrowed it from clever Robert) presence of Auntie Betty.

Mum and I were busy in the kitchen putting the final touches to our Christmas meal when she walks in and declares that such a spread is unpatriotic! I could have killed her and I am sure Mum felt the same, but Dad very sensibly replied that since rationing would come soon we might as well make the most of what we have and enjoy our food and drink.

So we all sit down and start stuffing ourselves except for Auntie Betty who sits very stiffly and barely touches the food that Mum had put on her plate. Robert elbows me in the ribs and mutters something about her having stuck a broomstick in her you-know-what. I burst out laughing and nearly choke on my turkey and as all eyes are turned on me gasping for air, some of the meat disappears from Betty's plate. Doug was blamed but did I detect a slight bulge in her cheeks? Anyway, she relented and when the Christmas pudding came, she certainly had her fair share.

Fri 29 Dec

Dad is re-decorating the shop like a madman. I try to help by shifting the stock here and there so he can get on with his work while still being open for business, but it isn't easy. Some customers have been complaining about the smell of paint and turps and my standard reply is "What do you expect from a hardware store, a smell of roses?" they titter and call me cheeky, and so does Dad, but it is all very good-natured.

I asked Dad why all this hurry to sort the shop out, as it has been announced that men of his age won't be called up for war for a long time, if at all. Suddenly he became very serious

'Fact is Annie ... fact is that I have volunteered. Don't tell your mother yet.'

I gasped and he gave me a half smile, as if asking for my approval.

'You'd do anything to get away from Auntie Betty, wouldn't you?'

I teased him trying to be funny, but my heart sank at the prospect of him leaving.

'Why did you do it Dad?' I asked.

'I'll have to go sooner or later, I'd rather do it at a time of my choosing. Also, I was too young for the Great War so this is my chance to do something for my country.'

I could agree with you but why are you leaving us so soon Dad?

That was my father all over: a man with a heart of gold, a twinkle in his eye, a sense of humour but an even stronger sense of duty. He was tall and quite good looking, calm and reliable. He could easily put up with Mum's pretensions and smile about them. Of course, we knew he could cope with anything. But there was another side to him which quietly looked at the world and saw what lay there. He got the measure of the various old ladies that came to the shop asking for products for their home and easily flirted with them. He gave them all nicknames and I am afraid some of the more uptight dames would have been offended on hearing them.

However, he was invariably kind and friendly towards all our customers, even the stroppiest among them like Mr Cribbles or Mr Harrigan. He was especially popular with the neighbouring farmers because he could supply everything they needed and didn't object to the strong smell of manure that pervaded the shop when they came in.

He left everything in good order before he went off to war. New supplies were proudly displayed in the window

11

under the bunting with Union Jacks. Pity the effect was ruined by the strips of anti-shatter tape. However, the place was pristine and all the paperwork was in tidy shape. Dad guided me through it so that I would be able to run the business, hopefully with some help from Mum.

JANUARY

Mon 1st Jan 1940

NEW YEAR'S DAY

This morning we greeted one another with 'Happy New Year' but there was a certain lack of enthusiasm and Dad looked just a touch glum. At breakfast Mum tried to cheer everybody up with another loud 'Happy New Year' but Dad looked at her and said 'I hope it will be happy, Madge...I've volunteered for the war.'

Mum just stood there dumbstruck, the teapot in her hand still pouring tea in her full cup, then she startled 'Oh dear!' she said and I don't know whether referring to the spilled tea or to Dad's announcement.

'Crikey. Good show!' Robert goes with a glint in his eyes and I bet that he couldn't wait to tell his schoolmates that our Dad is a hero. Mum had in the meantime regained her wits and, in tears, had rushed over to hug Dad. Unfortunately, in doing so she stepped on Doug's paw and he yelped loudly, which set Auntie Betty off.

13

'No need for this high drama. He is just doing his duty' and to me 'And don't you think you can do as you please just because your father is away.' TYPICAL!

As you know, usually New Year's Day is meant to mark a new beginning but for us in some ways it marked an end to family life as we knew it. The next few days were taken over with preparation for Dad leaving and as Mum was swaying from bursts of activity to moments of depression, Auntie Betty relentlessly interfered. Dad sought refuge in the shop while the two women argued over the contents of his kitbag.

It goes without saying that Betty won every encounter.

Thurs 4 Jan

Surprises never stop. In the past couple of days Robert has actually been in the shop, helping to decorate. Clever little so and so has come up with a ruse to get away from Auntie Betty.

Either that or he's feeling that Dad's departure will give him a different role in the family. Fact is that rather than lounging about with his "Oh, I am studying so hard" air, he has rolled up his sleeves and grabbed a paintbrush. It is like he is having a father-and-son time with Dad perhaps for the first time in his life.

When is he going to have a brother-and-sister time and help ME?

That was part of the problem with Robert. He had always been my mother's favourite and never really connected with Dad. Even the few occasions when they had been kicking a football together had been somewhat spoiled by my mother's jealous anxiety about his wellbeing. He had been rather sickly as a small child, "delicate" as she put it and it never occurred to her that he played on that to avoid any unpleasant work.

Robert's angelic good looks hid a good deal of craftiness and an impish sense of humour which could be quite endearing. His obvious cleverness and my mother's social ambitions had persuaded her to let him out of her sight as a day boarder at Albany Court.

Once he was out of her jealous gaze for most of the day, it was discovered that he had an unerring eye for catching a cricket ball thrown at high speed. In short, he became a much admired column of the school's cricket team and developed quite a following.

I loved my little brother, but what really got me was that I was expected to help in the shop and also to do my bit around the house while he, once home, lounged about claiming to be exhausted after a long day at school.

Things haven't changed much since then and us women are still lumbered with housework. Well, not actresses of course. I bet Suzie bloody Bell never had to sully her pretty little hands with cleaning a toilet, even before becoming a film star.

Sat 6 Jan

Oh My! Mum came back from the War Committee meeting all excited with a BIG piece of news. A whole regiment is to be stationed in this area and some of us might be asked to provide billets. Can you imagine it? Dashing soldiers and officers in smart uniforms in our backwater. Also, we will be hosting some children evacuated from areas at risk of bombing.

However not everybody is happy about the arrivals, Auntie Betty for one. She immediately gave me a lecture about behaving properly and not encouraging familiarities (as she put it) especially with Dad going away. Obviously, her patriotic fervour does not extend to welcoming the soldiers. I would not be surprised if she unleashed Doug on any coming too close to me. The poor chap would be nipped to death!

Later I shared the news with Peg. She called the arrival of the soldiers "a gift from the three wise kings" adding that they would bring more life to Millside.

However, as it later turned out, the three kings were not so wise. I think the soldiers did bring more life to our village, in more than one sense, as we had our own little baby boom the following year. Of course, it was in part attributed to the passionate embraces of the soon-to-depart-for-war husbands, but I still have some doubts....

Peg Fletcher was the daughter of the postmistress and my best friend. Her mother, a middle-aged widow lumbered with a disabled son, was rather strict with the girl. Peg could not wait to get out of her sight and, in a little village, the surest way was to find a man to marry.

The problem was that our rather restricted society did not offer many choices. To tell the truth Peg was very sweet on Gorgeous George, the village's mechanic and dashing captain of Millside's cricket team. Unfortunately, he was very popular with all the girls and, as the saying goes, he could have his pick among them, so Peg did not have much of a chance. Not that she was plain, but she did not stand out in a crowd, with her curly brown hair and slightly upturned nose. She was a little plump and showed already a woman's body, strangely at odds with her childish expression.

We had been friends since we were small and I really liked her sense of fun and the liveliness she displayed whenever she was out of her mother's disapproving stare. She was naturally open, trusting and friendly.

While us youngsters, most shopkeepers and not a few married women welcomed the idea of seeing new faces, some of the older residents went around looking sourer than ever. The Vicar himself was in some anxiety, as a guardian of morals and as the father of a teenage girl. Evidently in some people, like in Auntie Betty, patriotism and prejudice fought the first battle of this war.

However, prejudice was not limited to the presence of soldiers. The impending arrival of "scruffy urchins from the

17

slums of London" also fed into the worries of the older villagers who feared a complete disruption of their way of life. But that's war for you!

Me, I was not bothered by the forthcoming "invasion" of the evacuees. Little kiddies were of no interest to me, or so I thought.

Mon 8 Jan

This is it. From today we are officially on rations and bacon, butter and sugar are going to be very scarce. We can say goodbye to lovely Sunday breakfast and this isn't the only thing I am saying goodbye to.

This morning I was, as usual, helping Dad to open the shop as Master Robert was on his way to his posh school and Mum was puzzling over the new ration books. Billy Fletcher came from the post office with an envelope for Dad.

'S-something for you Mr. C-Corbett' he announced in his squeaky voice and his usual would-be-endearing grin. Poor Billy! People laugh at him because of his lame leg and his stammer but I sort of feel sorry for him. This however did not prevent me from slapping his hand hard when he tried to grope me as Dad was busy reading his letter. Now, if it had been Gorgeous George, who knows...

'That's it then' Dad said 'It's up to you now Annie. I have received my marching orders.'

And it was really up to me. Thank goodness Dad had left everything in order at our shop. It took the whole ground floor and part of the basement and we lived in the two upper floors. The house wasn't very big but it was comfortable. It had a garden which had been nice but with the war looming had been converted into a vegetable patch. The lawn had been given over to potatoes and cabbages and the summer house had been dismantled in favour of the Anderson shelter. Those awful corrugated iron shacks were meant to be buried in the gardens under three feet of soil, so that people could take refuge in them during bombing raids. We didn't really need one, as we had our own basement to shelter in, but my father thought that staying next to a stockroom full of chemicals, paints and other highly flammable products was not a good idea.

Mind you, the same had happened to everybody. Mrs Bassett, whose garden backed onto ours, was forever going on about the loss of her rose bed and even when complimented on the healthiness of her leeks commented sadly 'It is not the same'.

Apart from that, she wasn't at all a moany type. She had lost her husband in the Great War but widowhood had not soured her. Rather, it had made her quite maternal towards us youngsters and it wasn't uncommon for us to go to her with our problems. She seemed to have a smile, a good word and a cup of tea for everybody.

Weds 10 Jan

This morning Dad said it would be good for Mum to start helping in the shop before he left, as she had never taken much interest in it, lucky her!

So Mum comes down all ready for action. Whoops! She was wearing her best flowery frock and high heels. What was she expecting, the War Committee ladies to pop in for a cup of tea? Me, I was in my detested pale green overall and plimsolls, so much more practical for going up and down the ladder to reach the upper shelves. Poor Mum, she doesn't have a clue. However, she said she could help with the bills and orders. That would be great.

I was so judgemental then. In reality my mother had tried to help in the shop before but she had never been very good at it. I remember the infamous Plaster Disaster which involved stroppy Mr. Harrigan. He was a builder and decorator who lived about 3 miles away from Millside and was the most miserable, penny-pinching old codger of the whole community.

He had come to the shop and had asked for three and a half pounds of plaster. The plaster powder is very fine and has got to be handled carefully. Mum was so nervous that she dropped the scoop and the plaster flew everywhere. It was in her nose, in her hair and on every surface in a four feet radius, which of course included Mr Harrigan. He stomped out covered in the white stuff, looking like a ghost and my mother swore she would never set foot in the shop again.

Basically, she saw it as an essentially male environment and while she could relate to cleaning products she was not at ease with tools or bolts and certainly not with plaster. It is not that she was completely useless but like most women of her generation and her background she was held back in a well-defined role.

Sun 14 Jan

I am so proud of my Dad.

This morning at church the Vicar announced to everybody that Dad was leaving for the war tomorrow. He called him "our heroic volunteer" and all the congregation stood up as to salute him. As we left church the Vicar, the Headmaster and even Mr Cribbles came to shake Dad's hand before Alf dragged him to his pub for a few free drinks. The Vicar's wife was being especially nice to Mum and even Grace was trying to be nice to me. Pity they were both wearing the same fake smile.

Afterwards at home we spent our last afternoon with Dad playing card games and having a sing song with Mum at the piano (she is that refined). Auntie Betty, who had reluctantly joined in, put a stop to the fun by switching on the wireless. It was only hearing the news that Dad's departure hit us all. For once, the blots on this page are just tears.

It was a very sad ending for a day that had been happy in many different ways. Dad had come home from the pub rather flushed from the drinks and for having struck a deal with Alf, the landlord. In exchange for a tidy sum he had lent Alf his van for the duration of the war. It was a shrewd move as none of us could drive and the money would make up for a possible fall in profit from the shop. Having sorted us out moneywise, my father had felt free to indulge us with silly games to have the memory of a happy family afternoon to take with him in battle. We played Snap and Old Maid and every childhood game we knew and then Mum sat at the piano and away we went with old favourites like *Wish me Luck* and *Roll out the Barrel* until Auntie Betty's sobering interruption.

Not that she was completely wrong. The wireless, the radio as we say today, was our main form of entertainment and information. Nearly every family had a set and they would gather around it for the latest news about the war effort. Of course, all bulletins were strictly controlled and between censorship and propaganda, I doubt we got a realistic picture of what was going on. However positive news, cheerful songs and funny programmes helped people to look to an uncertain future with a smile on their faces.

Mon 15 Jan

This morning, thanks to Mum's War Committee contacts, none less than Miss Harriet Mandeville came to drive Dad to the District Recruitment Centre in her car.

I must admit I was a little tearful and so was Mum, although she tried to hold herself back before Harriet. Robert, who had skipped school to say goodbye to Dad kept reassuring him that he would look after us, being now the man of the house. I found this both funny and moving, but what was not funny was Auntie Betty sternly telling Dad off for wasting time. Dad looked grim for a moment but then his face relaxed in a smile and he said she would do better to tell Doug off: the nasty little mutt had piddled all over Harriet's tyre.

He picked up his bag and got in. As the car drove away I felt this sudden emptiness inside me, as if in the pit of my stomach there was a Dad-shaped void that nobody and nothing could fill until he came back.

PLEASE DAD, COME BACK SAFELY!

As soon as Dad left a convoy of Army trucks passed by. Some soldiers waved at us but I was too sad to wave back.

The Right Honourable Harriet Mandeville, daughter of the Lord of the Manor Francis Mandeville and member of the War Committee was not half as snobbish as that distinguished body. In fact, she was occasionally seen in the High Street passing the time of the day with us commoners and also occasionally, scandal of scandals, IN THE PUB. She was an attractive brunette who wore stylish clothes which looked as if they were new. And she even smelled good, with a waft of enticing Parisian perfume. No wonder men would do anything for her, either for her charm or her status, and that included Mr Cribbles. She careered around the country in her sports car and at times she would stop and offer a lift to old ladies returning from the shops. In a few words, she was kind, sociable and not at all stuffy.

Thurs 18 Jan

THE BRATS ARE COMING

After the last War Committee meeting Mum was told by Mrs Fletcher to prepare lists of possible hosts for the evacuees that are due to arrive next Sunday. Every family in Millside has been asked to take one or more. As we already have an evacuee, Auntie Betty (ha, ha!) we will be kept in reserve for possible changes. Just as well, we already have enough disruption in our lives as it is.

To house evacuees was not strictly compulsory but if you were chosen to act as a host you could not really say no, especially if you lived in a large house. Billeting officers put together lists of hosts and had the power to fine people who refused to play their part. Mrs Fletcher, being the post mistress, was the natural choice for the job.

Of course, host families did not do it for free. The Government paid good money for looking after the children and it happened that sometimes even families living in tiny places would offer to take them in, as a way to get extra cash. So, some evacuees were lucky enough to live in mansions while others had to make do with a bed under the stairs. Some children were hosted by loving and caring people, whatever the standard of accommodation, while others were barely tolerated. Some unscrupulous individuals even pocketed the evacuees' ration books to fill their own bellies and got away with it.

But of course we did not know anything about this. What we got from the wireless were reports of happy children being made welcome everywhere by friendly faces. The evacuees themselves had been told that they were going "for a nice holiday in the country", the only downside being that they were not allowed to take their favourite toys. Newspapers were printing only pictures of smiling youngsters and cutting out any tearful faces.

The same occurred in the newsreels that accompanied films. They were carefully edited in order to present images of a well-organised, proud country whose people faced a war with courage and a sense of togetherness.

Sun 21 Jan

After lunch despite the wet weather we all marched to the Farmers' Hall for the evacuees' arrival. Everybody was there, including some farmers that didn't show their faces in the village very often. As usual Mr. Cribbles was trying to take over and stood there in his tin hat, feeling very important but to me he just looked ridiculous.

We waited and waited and eventually two lorries arrived and unloaded a large number of cold, miserable looking children. They stood in a group, clutching their bundles and gas masks while people were staring at them. It felt a bit like being in a cattle market and it got even worse. Before Mum could even pull out her lists, some of the farmers elbowed out Cribbles and made a grab for the stouter boys. Other hosts just pulled away from the bunch the kids they fancied better and at the end of the scrum there was only a small blond boy left, a sad little figure standing all alone in the middle of the floor.

Not for long. Mr Harrigan, him of the Plaster Disaster, grabbed the boy roughly by the arm saying 'Come along, scrap. What's your name?' The answer was just a frightened whisper 'Ben'.

Poor kid. Harrigan is a stroppy bossy boots and his wife is no better!

The day of the evacuees' arrival was bitterly cold. The telegram to the post office said to expect 20 youngsters but more arrived. They looked scruffy and exhausted. There had been a mix-up over the transport and they had to bunk up in the officers' quarters at Newbury.

A thoughtful suggestion by Harriet that the evacuees should join us for a Sunday service in the church had to be dropped because they arrived late.

In the end they were set down at the Farmers' Hall, a short walk from the village. It had a small stage at the end and a tiny kitchen with a tea-making urn. The hall had been put up 30 years earlier thanks to the donations of the Barons of Wheat, to acknowledge the substantial amount of grain which was grown and ground around Millside.

On that cold, dull day it didn't look particularly welcoming nor, I must admit, did the villagers. Maybe the long wait had dampened any enthusiasm, but some people saw hosting as an unpleasant duty, while others seemed to be more willing to take in the evacuees as a way of cutting a good figure in the community. Luckily there were also many well-intentioned, kind-hearted people like Mrs Bassett. She took in two naughty but nice twin sisters from the London slums. The first thing she did for them was to give them both a good scrub, a good meal and a big hug, which made all the difference. Pity that a few days afterward their heavily pregnant mother came to fetch them back to help with the coming baby.

Some of the keenest hosts were farmers eager to get their hands on cheap labour. Unfortunately, one of them found that the sturdy lad he had grabbed as an unpaid farm hand had no intention to act the part and, when threatened with "a good whipping" had actually pushed the farmer into the dunghill and run away. A few hours later he was found stranded near the Manor by Harriet Mandeville who, on hearing his story, persuaded the pub landlord to take him in, a much more successful placement for a city boy.

Mon 22 Jan

Now, this is strange. I was just outside the shop when I saw Grace walking around with a new girl, smiling right and left with her usual superior air, just like a princess on a walkabout. They came towards me and Grace introduced the girl 'This is Elsa, our evacuee'.

'Welcome to Millside' I said and Elsa smiled and held out her hand. She's very pretty, well dressed and, as I could see, well mannered. Strange that I didn't notice her in the Farmers' Hall yesterday.

Later Mum came up with an explanation. Grace's mother had spotted her on arrival and noticed how well presented she was. Without any by-your-leave she had '"appropriated" her as a suitable companion for Grace.

No riffraff for the Cummings household!

A lot of people acted like that. Despite the claims that all children were equal in the eyes of the evacuation authorities, at local level some children were more equal than others when it came to allocations. The better dressed, better mannered ones were earmarked as first choice and very desirable guests.

Thurs 25 Jan

This morning Billy brought a letter from Dad! He's alright and has started his training as a driver - after that some words were blacked out. He says he misses us all even Auntie Betty (but not as much as I miss him, I'm sure). He said next time he would send us a photo. I can't wait to see him in his uniform.

Later Mrs Harrigan popped into the shop to buy some paint brushes. I think her husband isn't happy with Dad not being here to serve him.

Anyway, she had the little blond boy by her side. He was pale and had an anxious look about him. I greeted him with a friendly hallo but he didn't answer.

'Where's yer manners' Mrs Harrigan barked at him.

The boy jumped and whispered

'Hallo Miss'.

'Not miss, my name is Annie, what's your name?'

'Ben'.

I got closer and made as if to muss his hair and he flinched as if afraid. Then Mrs Harrigan dragged him out of the shop. Poor kid. Why isn't he at school?

As it happens, Millside was trying to return to some sort of normality and the evacuees had been found places in the local school which now operated in two shifts. Half the pupils, old and new, would attend in the morning and the other half in the afternoon. To make up for the shortened school day homework was doubled, much to the annoyance of the young layabouts and of the mums that had to supervise them at home. The only winners in this situation were some hosts that didn't give a hoot about the kids' schooling and homework and had them at their service for most of the day. I suspected that the Harrigans belonged to this sort.

Sat 27 Jan

My Mum has really surprised me. She has managed to organise a trip to the cinema in the nearest town for us youngsters. It was her idea as she said we deserved a treat.

We gathered outside the pub and Gorgeous George came along driving Dad's van. (Dad, I miss you so much!). We all squeezed in, even Grace Cummings and her brother. I thought going in a van would be beneath her but the attraction of the cinema was too strong for her and Philip. He normally keeps his nose in his books but this was a treat not to be missed. I suddenly realised that the new girl Elsa wasn't with us and I asked about her. Grace's face closed up as she replied that Elsa had seen the film already in London. Anyway, off we went - and of course Billy managed to pinch my bottom as I got in. We were out for most of the afternoon at the fleapit in Hungerford. We watched *The Wizard of Oz*. It was GREAT and we also had some sweets to go with it!

On the way back we were singing songs from the film and George kept telling us to pipe down as he had to concentrate on driving with dipped lights because of the blackout.

We were still merry and we were nearly home but all the fun stopped when the air raid sirens went off and we had to get out of the van and lay down in the ditch. I found myself beside Grace, we were sandwiched between Robert and Philip and they both kept telling us not to be afraid. Anyway we reached home covered in mud - I wouldn't be surprised to find a frog in my knickers.

I must give my mother credit - she had organised a nice surprise for us. She had talked Alf into lending the van and persuaded George to take the afternoon off to drive us to the cinema. Bravo Mum!

I was sitting at the front and I almost imagined Dad was driving, it was the sort of thing he used to do. Therefore for me this trip was bittersweet, you know what it's like when nostalgia creeps in.

So my mood was slightly spoiled. And of course it was spoiled for everybody when the siren came. We heard the sound of an explosion far away and we thought 'what if it had hit the cinema!'. We lifted ourselves from the ditch and huddled back in the van - wet, cold and miserable, although I must admit I took a perverse pleasure in pushing Grace's face in the mud. There, I said it folks!

My dislike of Grace didn't extend to Philip. He was slightly older than us and about to go to university. He was tall, wore spectacles and had an absent-minded air that had a sort of charm. He didn't make much of sheltering in the ditch but us girls were moaning about our ruined dresses, especially Peg. It was well-known that she didn't own many clothes as her mother wouldn't spend any unnecessary money on her.

I know now that we were actually quite lucky as children in Millside during the war. We were a tight-knit community and well-off compared to others. Later we heard about how young people had suffered in the cities - some literally bringing themselves up in families where the father was at war and the mother was working all day in the ammunitions factories.

Although my father had gone off to the front, there were plenty of familiar faces at home who continued to keep an eye on us, as Millside was an old-fashioned village. And while the farmers and some of their wives could seem occasionally grumpy, their activities on the land did mean that we had a lot more country food off the rations than people who lived in cities like London and Birmingham and were going hungry.

We followed the seasons and customs through the year, expecting the range of travelling vendors who were still calling at our doors at fixed points. Even the war wouldn't deter the visits from the umbrella repair man or the knick knack seller who now arrived in their horse and cart.

Sun 28 Jan

Today during the service the Vicar announced that we are to offer our baths to the arriving soldiers. Robert whispered a vicar should be more interested in cleansing souls rather than bodies. Anyway those of us who are fortunate enough to have bathrooms are invited to put them to our "brave warriors' disposal". He added that of course the bathrooms would have to be sparkling and would anybody volunteer to inspect them. Immediately Mr Cribbles' hand shot up like a firework.

'You can leave it to ME and I'll make sure no-one will disgrace Millside.' TYPICAL! Once again Peg's eyes lit up. I bet she wasn't thinking about the cleaning bit but rather about handsome soldiers with their kit off, if you know what I mean. Me, practical as ever, was thinking about checking our stock of bath cleaning stuff. How sad to be so commonplace! And that is not all. The families that don't have "proper bathrooms" are asked to take in the servicemen's washing to be returned clean a week later. Every family will be given a bundle of dirties from the same man each week.

Mr Cribbles did not waste time. I remember that as soon as the service was over he started poking his nose around the village to check if the few available bathrooms were fit for purpose. No tin baths in the kitchen for our young heroes, but proper bathtubs with running water. We were lucky enough to have one of those and so we were one of his first targets. My mother had no time to spare for him and so Auntie Betty took over. What a sight! Cribbles, nose in the air and silly moustache vibrating, was pontificating on the standards to be observed in terms of bathroom quality. Opposite him, Betty's mousy hairdo was vibrating in sympathy, as she nodded in agreement to his every word. In short, our bathroom just passed the test and my aunt reassured him that he wouldn't find anything amiss on his next inspection. 'I would not expect anything less from YOU Miss Betty' he replied and, would you believe it, she blushed.

We did not get any washing to do but other families did, including Peg's. Occasionally the clothes were returned to the soldiers with little additions, a pack of cigarettes, some sweets or even a secret love letter.

Tues 30 Jan

Dad has left but servicemen have arrived everywhere. It seems that the Manor is being used to house officers and temporary barracks are being built nearby. Good luck to Lord Francis, but I am sure that Harriet will enjoy their company. Will this make us more of a target for Jerry bombers? For sure we are having our share of air raid alarms and I HATE the blooming Anderson shelter! It may save us but being in it is like being buried alive.

After my father's departure, events seem to speed up. We'd already been invaded by our own soldiers, so to speak and the next development was an announcement that the Manor House was to be commandeered. Home to Harriet and her father Lord Francis Mandeville, it was a gracious building with 10 bedrooms set slightly aside from Millside. It had been given a more modern look before the Great War but after the death of Lady Mandeville in the early 30's had reverted to a state of slight abandonment that not even Harriet's energy could alter.

The Manor House used to have a team of servants, but the war meant the butler and the footmen had left to join up and Jimmy the groom had been let go. Some of the rooms had been shut up and the furniture covered. Once they were re-opened and aired it was the obvious place for officers to be billeted.

Harriet joked she was happy to accommodate the officer class. However her father, who was more of a recluse, accepted reluctantly that it was in the interest of everyone if the large house was made use of.

He was a rather distinguished figure, tall and slim with a pale whiskered face. He was rarely seen in the village itself and was said to spend time in his library with a glass of port reliving former glories.

Now he would have to leave his comfortable isolation and rub shoulders with men from different walks of life. Gone were the days when officers were mostly members of the upper classes – World War Two was proving to be a great social leveller.

FEBRUARY

Thurs 1st Feb

HOORAY FOR HARRIET

The past three days have been really hard. Not only missing Dad like mad, but also having to deal with both Mum and Auntie Betty. Mum is trying to be helpful, fine. Auntie Betty is trying to take over, as per usual. So, what am I moaning about? Well, the two dears are on a joint mission: keeping an eye on a "fatherless daughter" as Betty puts it. It's true that most of our customers are men, but I am not really in danger of being seduced by any of the old codgers that come to our shop.

To cap it all Robert, in his new role as the man of the house is now sitting in Dad's place at the dinner table!

Luckily in all this doom and gloom there is a piece of brilliant news. Harriet Mandeville is going to organise a dance in the Farmers' Hall to which the soldiers will also be invited, to keep up people's morale. It certainly has done wonders for mine!

Our morale did need keeping up. England was in the grip of an extremely cold spell which added to the general misery of war. It was so cold that the Thames itself had frozen over and the messages on the wireless to save fuel for the war effort made us feel even colder. The idea of a dance was all the more welcome as a way of bringing us both fun and warmth.

We were all quite excited and Peg was over the moon. Here was the chance to meet young men who could become husband material.

Unfortunately, her eagerness to escape her mother's clutches had a downside. Peg could become an easy prey for any young man with a good chat line and a handsome face, as she had proved with Jimmy, the Manor House groom. The young rascal had taken her fancy by arriving at the post office on a horse to collect Lord Francis's weekly magazine. She could not resist the lure of this "knight in a shiny waistcoat" and some serious smooching had gone on behind the counter.

As bad luck would have it, Peg's mother caught them and lashed out at them both. Then she marched to the Manor House and demanded Jimmy's dismissal. Lord Francis, being very old-fashioned, agreed and the whole story was hushed up.

Sat 3 Feb

Early this morning that old busybody Mr. Cribbles descended on us for the bathroom inspection. Mum was all in a flutter and so, as it turned out, was Auntie Betty. I was getting ready to open the shop but decided to stay to support them and even Robert got out of bed ready to defend the honour of the Corbett's bathroom.

Cribbles sniffed around, touched surfaces and tested taps but could not find anything to criticise (Batty Betty had been very busy). He looked a little crestfallen but suddenly his face lit up. 'You haven't got the line' he said. 'What line?' Mum asked timidly. 'Don't you listen to the wireless? To waste hot water is unpatriotic. The maximum recommended is 3 inches of hot water and that must be marked by a line painted in the bathtub' and to me 'Young lady, go to the shop and fetch a tin of enamel paint and a thin brush.' THE CHEEK!

Bernard Cribbles made life difficult for the rest of us because he was a self-important, interfering fusspot. Being the Air Raid Precautions Warden meant he was having the time of his life. He would stalk round the village at night searching for the tiniest chink of light flashing from a blackout curtain. He would rap on the unfortunate resident's door and bark 'Put that light out!' before making a meticulous note of the wrongdoer in his government-issue notebook.

So his high-handed way in the bathroom inspection did not come as a surprise but what WAS surprising was the reaction of Auntie Betty. Rather than being outraged at his rude telling off she kept going along with what he was saying and nodding at him.

In a way they were similar, if they thought things were wrong they took it as a personal affront. They were obsessed with doing the right thing and were always nitpicking and finding faults.

Sun 4 Feb

Well, what do you know! With all the excitement of last Sunday's announcement about the baths most people, me among them, did not notice Elsa wasn't there. But today it was impossible to miss. People started wondering and also remembered that they hadn't seen her with Grace around the village.

Mrs Stone, as nosey as ever, went straight to the Vicar's wife and asked about Elsa. Mrs Cummings looked embarrassed and just said that the girl had gone away as she couldn't fit in with the family. I think this is very strange, as she seemed so nice and Grace seemed quite taken with her.

The real explanation emerged a few days later. Elsa couldn't fit in a religious household, as Mrs Cummings put it, because she was Jewish. It is not that they were racists or antisemitic, oh no. It was just that a Vicarage was definitely not the best place for her and, had they known….and so on and so forth.

I think they were regretting their hasty grab of the best dressed, best mannered girl and were at a loss about what to do but fortunately Harriet Mandeville once again came to the rescue. A few well-aimed phone calls secured a place for Elsa with a Jewish family in Hungerford.

Although the problem was happily resolved, it was another sign that the evacuation wasn't as smooth as it was portrayed and that more attention to the children's background would have helped.

Tues 6 Feb

The first uniforms are around in the village. We haven't had our "bather" yet, but it won't be long. In the meantime I saw something rather special. I was in the back garden checking the Anderson shelter. This was normally Dad's job and I was feeling really miserable. Anyway, this soldier comes out of Mrs Bassett's house. He was carrying a pile of wet washing and helped her to hang it out saying 'I have given you more washing to do so it's only fair I help you with this lot'.

What a nice thing to do! I don't know why, but it made me feel better. Mrs Bassett called me over 'Annie, come and meet Private Russell.' I went to the fence and saw that Private Russell had the bluest eyes I've ever seen.

And that's not all, later on that same soldier popped into the shop and he was surprised at seeing me. 'Oh, hallo Miss Annie' he said. 'Hallo Private

Russell' I replied. 'Just Remy, Remy Russell if you don't mind." He smiled and the whole world lit up.

Remy was an unusual name, that is, unusual for us. As it turned out, he was half French and was being trained to join the British Expeditionary Force in France as an interpreter. He was quite tall and so good-looking, with very dark hair and that winning smile. Although he had just turned nineteen, he had all the self-confidence that comes with moving between two different cultures. As the war loomed he had delayed going to University in order to join the army: he would fight for Britain until the moment came to fight for France. While waiting for his moment he enjoyed the camaraderie of the army, could laugh about its drawbacks and was relaxed in most situations. Often he could get around problems with the easy charm which had already worked its magic on Mrs Bassett and, may I add, on me.

Thurs 8 Feb

Today Billy brought us another letter from Dad. We'd been worried because we hadn't received anything for two weeks but this letter made up for the wait because in it there was a picture of him. How nice he looks in his uniform! (nearly as nice as a certain soldier...).

He writes that he is well but he misses us all and misses Mum's cooking. Well, perhaps he hasn't faced food rationing yet. The Army's cooks must have more food in their stores but they aren't as good as Mum.

Mum was over the moon with the letter and the picture and she showed it to everybody and anybody until Betty told her to stop showing off. Betty had to eat her words though, as Harriet Mandeville asked Mum to pin the photo on the committee notice board for a few days as a public acknowledgment of Dad volunteering for the war. She did so and quite a lot of ladies complimented her on how handsome he looked, which made her feel proud and, for once, important.

Sun 11 Feb

This morning in church the congregation was bigger, as it included many evacuees. Among the new faces I spotted the little blond kid, Ben. My heart went out to him as he looked quite miserable, wedged in between the Harrigans. He was pale and drawn-looking. Are they feeding him properly? I know we are on rations, but yet...

Anyway, after the service Peg and I went for a stroll in the High Street which was bustling with servicemen. Peg's eyes were darting here and there taking in all those handsome young men showing off in their new uniforms. Well, so were mine until I spotted Mrs. Bassett's Remy. He saw me too and started to move towards me but one of his pals dragged him towards the pub. What a pity. I could fall for that smile.

I didn't know it yet, but I had already fallen. Remy was …Remy

He and his friend made an unlikely pair. One tall, slim and dark haired, with a natural elegance and that smile. The other a little stocky with sandy hair and a booming laugh. He also seemed to have an eye for the ladies and when we saw him later he winked at Peg and cheekily blew her a kiss.

In fact, a lot of Tommies seemed to wink at the Millside ladies, the sound of wolf whistles following some of them. You know what groups of young men are like.

Not even Auntie Betty escaped their attentions, as she indignantly told us. Robert and I wondered if she would have reacted like that if an officer had approached her. It would've taken a real hero to do so. It would've been a Saint George and the dragon situation, with Betty in the part of the dragon.

Mon 12 Feb

Today Sergeant Stuart Higgins came in for his bath. He is fairly good looking, with wavy brown hair smothered in Brylcreem and a thin moustache. He is polite, if a little arrogant, but there is something about him that makes me slightly uncomfortable. I think he fancies himself a lot and

that's reason enough for me not to fancy him.
(Anyway he isn't a patch on that soldier Remy).

Mum however seems to like him and Auntie Betty
is somewhat reassured by my evident lack of
interest, so she's keeping Doug on the leash.

Sergeant Higgins started to come for his weekly bath and each time he and my mother would spend a few minutes together over a cup of tea. He was definitely a ladies' man and whenever he came across me, Mum, Auntie Betty or any female visitor he would look at us with a slight smile bordering on a smirk, while smoothing his moustache. I found him unbearable and so did Robert, but we were the only ones to positively dislike him.

As for all the other soldiers that were descending on Millside for bathing and washing facilities (or for visiting newly found lady friends) their presence was seen as a sort of necessary evil by some of the villagers and as a source of much needed cash by the pub landlord and by us shopkeepers.

And some of the ladies, well, our young men were being called up to join the Army and loneliness is very bad for your morale. What a good excuse for a bit of flirting with a handsome serviceman.

Weds 14 Feb

VALENTINE'S DAY

The big day is getting nearer! The whole village seems to be readying itself for the dance. Of course Auntie Betty is set against me going but, as the dance has been organised by Harriet Mandeville, Mum has no qualms about it, even if she won't be going herself. In fact Mum has offered to lend me one of her dresses and her best shoes. Pity they pinch my toes, but they are smart. Mum has a fuller figure than me but the dress can be adapted quickly.

And, by the way, I DID receive a Valentine card. Only, it was from Billy. I would recognise his wobbly handwriting anywhere. Unfortunately it has come from the WRONG BOY!

The village had always had a positive approach to community life and the dance was no exception. The months leading up to the war and the start of the fighting had worried and depressed the people of Millside and there hadn't been any fun at all, so it was time for us to get in the mood. Strings of bunting flags were pulled out of dusty cupboards in the church hall and pinned up around the Farmers' Hall. The village's youngsters made a real effort to clean it up and decorate it. The Christmas tinsel was pinned back up and paper chains were swiftly produced.

The old, battered tea urn itself was suddenly promoted to a grog-making facility.

Harriet Mandeville took care of the music by transporting her gramophone and records to the Hall. Even she could not really ask the regiment's band to play for us, nevertheless she helped us to make the most of the soldiers' presence and their beer supply. The soldiers also provided us with some snacks and treats from their own canteen, to make up for the rationing restrictions. Harriet typically took charge in her light-hearted yet confident way to provide us with an event which would change forever the lives of some of those who paid their tuppence to get in.

Sat 17 Feb

The big day is here. I'm wearing the pretty dress Mum has altered for me, and I feel very grown up and glamorous. As I go downstairs I am greeted by a stare of disapproval from Auntie Betty, a gape of surprise from Robert and a look of tender pride from Mum.

* * *

Peg and Billy came to fetch me. Of course Peg's mother wouldn't let her go anywhere without him. So, courtesy of the blackout, we trudged in the dark to the Farmers' Hall. On the door we shed our old coats together with our gas masks and walked in feeling a little bashful in such a crowd. Some farm boys sniggered at seeing poor, lame Billy at a dance but we ignored them and looked for more friendly faces.

A voice whispered "Would you care to dance Miss Annie?"

I turned around and saw Remy Russell smiling at me. He was with two soldiers that he introduced to us and while one started talking to Billy the other whisked Peg off on the dance floor. He was the stocky young man that had blown her a kiss in the street, Andrew Miller. As for me, I just smiled back and took Remy's arm. I had a lovely evening, of course I danced with different lads but Remy kept asking me and even bought me a drink, well, a lemonade. A table, set slightly apart, sat some officers, Harriet Mandeville, Philip and, to my annoyance, Grace Cummings looking all ladylike in a new frock and pearl earrings. I saw that Remy danced with her once and the little cat kept making eyes at him. Fortunately she didn't stay long and after the first few dances left with Philip, the officers and Harriett. PHEW!

He looked relieved. Evidently escorting his sister wasn't to his taste. He would've been happier at home with a book. But he gave me a wave as he went out of the door.

After that things warmed up and people started letting their hair down. Remy said how much he was enjoying dancing with me after the previous stuffy company (ha ha, Grace) and when I left he kissed my hand. So very French!

Billy stayed by the bar trying to talk to people (not easy with his stammer) but I must say I didn't see much of Peg until going home time and when I finally managed to track her she looked rather flushed. Was it just the heat of the dance? I am sure she will tell me everything tomorrow.

That dance, my first dance, is still etched in my memory. It was as if all the gloom and darkness of a winter at war had ceased to exist. Farmers' wives had dressed up and slapped on make up and even the committee ladies were letting themselves go. Well, there were just a few lamps and a gramophone with a limited number of records but the light and the music inside the hall made you forget all your worries. And certainly all the twirling on the dance floor made you forget the cold outside. Or even forget yourself, as the saying goes. There was a certain amount of smooching going on in dark corners and more than one probing hand was slapped away. Not by me, I must say. Remy was very charming and kind and my other partners were generally alright.

As for my companions, Billy had been bought a few beers and was rather dizzy while Peg's dizziness was down to other reasons, as it emerged.

Sun 18 Feb

Aah, Sunday! It is nice not to have to get up early and open shop, especially after yesterday evening. I did SO enjoy myself and so did everybody else. I am sure Mum would've loved to come as well but could not face Auntie Betty's disapproval. Anyway, it was funny to see a few of our customers letting their hair down. Even stuck-up Mrs Bellows was there and what's more, she seemed to be flirting with an airman. Mmm. The soldiers were getting most of the attention and putting the local boys in the shade, except for our Gorgeous George. Mind you, Remy was more than a match for him.

Oh, here comes Peg

* * *

My oh my, naughty Peg! Not only did she dance all evening, smoked a cigarette and drank a glass of sherry, she was also kissed by TWO different soldiers and not on the hand either. Why two, I asked and she simply replied that she didn't like the first one, so she decided to try again with Andrew Miller and this time it was much better. Her Mum would have a fit if she knew.

SHE DID!!! Too tired to write more.

Peg had been determined to have a good time that evening. Her brother was foisted on us in the walk up to the Farmers' Hall but when we arrived, she soon found other company. It was as if she knew she had a limited amount of time to meet new people. She'd been excited for days and while she loved Billy, she wanted to be a normal young woman for once. Her youth and freshness made up for the odd-looking pattern on her dress. Most women had faced the issue of "make do and mend" but some could sew and choose styles better than others but not Peg. However, she was soon twirling with her soldier with a cigarette in her hand. She had lots of energy and I could see some of the married women watching her with a touch of envy. Peg's dancing sparked off others and they were quickly caught up in the restless swirl of movement.

One of the first to approach the ladies was Gorgeous George. He was handsome and confident - he knew he would never be turned down. He'd found a smart though rather heavy blue suit from somewhere and even had a spotted red and white hankie in his breast pocket. Soon he got rid of the jacket, showing braces and his muscular arms, with a trickle of sweat down the back of his white shirt while he partnered one of the prettier wives to the music.

How quickly they all let themselves go - as if all the worry about the war just melted away.

There were a surprisingly large number of women whose husbands had gone off to the army - well, that's how it seemed. Word must have got round about the dance for miles. They might have been respectably wed but they had still made a huge effort to look nice with hair in the wartime Victory Rolls which the magazines were featuring. They all wore their favourite brand of lipstick and some of them even had perfume. Mind you, those delicate scents were soon overwhelmed by the smell of cigarettes, beer and male sweat - British soldiers hadn't yet discovered deodorant like their American counterpart.

Mon 19 Feb

What an uproar!

Yesterday at the end of the Sunday service the vicar asked if there were any more notices. Mr Cribbles stood up and launched a tirade against the people who, he said, had let the whole village down by misbehaving at the dance (the old so-and-so had been snooping around on the pretext of checking the blackout regulations). As he talked, he was staring at several people. At a certain point his beady eyes focused on Peg and Billy. Billy giggled in his silly way and elbowed her in the ribs as everyone stared at the pair of them. Peg blushed and their mother looked dumbstruck.

As we left church I could see her almost dragging them home. Good luck to them!

Cribbles didn't know it but he had opened a can of worms. Some of the women he had looked at would have some explaining to do.

As for Billy and Peg, they sheepishly followed their mother home where all hell broke loose.

Billy was castigated not only for getting drunk but also for failing to keep an eye on his sister. And Peg, well, she was treated like a lightskirt who had embarrassed her mother in front of the whole congregation and she was told that 'this was it' as far as the dances were concerned. Not only that, she would not be allowed to go out on her own. Peg wasn't mature enough to recognise this as an empty threat and resolved not to accept her mother's ruling.

Thurs 22 Feb

Haven't seen Peg since Sunday. I wonder whether she's in _serious_ trouble with her mum. I don't get much time to think about her as I'm very busy in the shop and I get precious little help. However, Mum has suggested we find somebody to help with the lifting and moving of heavy stuff and she will ask Mrs Fletcher if we can borrow Billy a couple of times a week.

P.S. I may not have much time to think about Peg but I find the odd moment to think about two _very_ blue eyes and a heart-stopping smile.... Mmmmm, Remy.

I forget everything for a while but then something else comes up: a sad little face under a thatch of blond hair.

What is happening to me? I seem to be always thinking about boys, although of different kinds and for different reasons.

Billy helping was the key to Peg coming out of seclusion. Her mother allowed her to come to the shop whenever Billy was working and things got back to nearly normal in the family. Unfortunately, some of our regular customers had been present when my friend and Billy came under Cribble's gaze and some snide comments were made. Peg appeared not to notice but inside she was angry. What made her mad was the unfairness of the situation. Okay, she'd been kissed by soldiers but that did not make her a tart and anyway kissing was very pleasant and no big matter after all.

And I must say kissing happened often in the shop in the following weeks. As if by chance one of Peg's soldiers, Andrew the one she'd liked better, popped in to buy odd things whenever Peg was there. Sometimes with Remy, sometimes on his own. Peg started to spend a lot of time with him in the storeroom and there were some strange noises coming from there when Billy was out on deliveries.

Sun 25 Feb

Well, I thought so.

Last night Mum came back from the War Committee meeting rather upset. There have been rumours that Ben, the little blond boy, is being mistreated by the Harrigans. They weren't in church today so after lunch Mum and Harriet Mandeville went to check the situation. Mum was really chuffed about having such an important role

AND being driven in Harriet's sports car. As for me,
I wish Dad had been with them. He certainly knows
how to deal with bullies like Joe Harrigan!

In reality, my mother had already noticed that Ben was
looking pale and weak and knew something was not right.
In the village the women would stand around discussing the
evacuees, expressing their concern and chewing over every
detail. As for me, I had no doubt they talked about the
Harrigans' home and that it was really the last place any
guest should go and certainly not a young child.

The Harrigans' did not really care about the community.
They showed their faces in church and that was it. Even
when they went to the shops they never stopped for a chat
or a gossip. In short, they were a cold, unsociable couple.
Obviously they had taken Ben in for the government
money, but they had not realised that a little boy's presence
would disrupt their staid routine. They largely ignored him,
if they talked to him at all it was just to tell him off and Mrs
Harrigan was not averse to deal him an occasional slap.

Tues 27 Feb

I HATE GRACE!

Today Remy came to the shop after his weekly bath
at Mrs. Bassett's. We were having a quiet moment
together when who walks in but blooming Grace
Cummings!

'Oh, it's you private Russell,' she cooed, as if she
hadn't planned to see him all along.

And to me, ' Can you get the big wicker basket in the window?'

She could at least say please!

As I went to grab it she started chatting Remy up and he was smiling at her and looking into her eyes!

I banged the basket on the counter, she gave me the money and made a show of struggling to hold it. Remy fell for it and offered to take it home for her. So he waved to me and away they went.

I COULD HAVE KILLED HER

With your first love, also comes your first love pangs and jealousy. In reality, Remy was just being a gentleman but at that moment it felt like a betrayal. The hero walks away with the princess leaving the handmaiden in the green overall behind. That was Remy, courteous to a fault, and yet…

As I was later to discover, his polite, easy ways hid steel in his character, as well as a rebellious streak. He would defy authority and face danger to put right what he saw as wrong.

This, as the war continued, led him to leave the relatively easy life of an interpreter and to become a secret agent working with the French Resistance in their fight against the Nazis.

Like many people of mixed background, his loyalties were divided. He loved Britain and was proud of his

English heritage and yet France held a special place in his heart. It was the land his mother came from and French were the first words he had heard as a baby. To him it represented all the love and warmth his mother had given him before her recent death and he would fight for it as he would for Britain.

MARCH

Fri 1st March

When Mum came home from the Committee today there was a little parcel from Dad waiting for her. In it there was a lovely face powder compact with a Valentine's heart on the lid. It was only two weeks late!

Anyway she opens the compact with trembling hands, it slips and falls to the floor cracking the mirror and spilling the contents. Poor Mum, she was SO upset and she burst into tears. She's definitely unlucky with powder!

The sad fate of what had been clearly intended as a Valentine gift was almost too much for my mother to bear. She kept going on about seven years of bad luck and 'What would your father think?' until Betty pulled her up,

'There are bigger problems, you know.'

And indeed there were, because our own little evacuee was about to arrive.

sun 3 March

This morning in church Grace was looking at me with such a smug face that I don't know how I kept my hands off her. Anyway there was worst to come. As we were leaving after the service the Harrigans blocked our way:

'So we're not good enough for the little b..., are we?' they growled, 'Well, you deal with him!' and shoved poor little Ben right into Mum while dumping his bag on the floor.

Mum rose to the challenge. "Clearly you are not,"she replied and taking Ben by the hand, she turned her back and walked out on them. We followed and Ben came home with us.

The rumours were right for once: he was being mistreated and so we're taking him in. He'll sleep in the little basement room. It opens onto mine which is annoying, but it'll be a safe place for him.

3 A.M.

What a night! Ben couldn't sleep and of course, neither could I. And I have a full day of work ahead.

As Ben walked through our door, he didn't say a word, just looked bewildered and only managed a smile when Doug came sniffing around him. That smile however, was very short-lived, due to the sharp nip he received. We showed him his room and helped him to sort out his things.

Not that there was much to sort, just some underwear, a change of clothes, his gas mask and a well-thumbed copy of Swallows and Amazons. As we picked it up, out came the picture of a sad-looking woman with a dog and a strikingly pretty teenage girl. For us the most important item was his ration book which Betty immediately grabbed.

Ben didn't talk much. Not during dinner nor when we sat around the wireless. He would answer in a whisper any questions we cared to ask but didn't offer any information. We only learned that he was eight and the women in the photo were his mother and his sister Suzie.

Bedtime came, he went quietly to his bed and I got into mine. Later in the night a slight snuffling noise woke me up. A mouse, I thought and got up to put the light on to scare it away. In the sudden glare I saw a little figure standing still in the doorway, a silent tear running down his cheek, looking absolutely forlorn. What could I do?

I went to him and he stepped back looking scared but I hugged him and I felt him give in a little bit. I took him back to his bed and stayed with him until he fell asleep.

In the morning I was slightly grumpy due to lack of sleep but I got on with my job. Chatting with the customers I discovered that our experience was barely unique and there had been quite a number of tearful kiddies moping around the village. The government portrayal of "Happy Children on a Happy Holiday" was mostly propaganda.

Mon 4 March

What a great announcement just before Easter. Meat is being rationed from next week. What about our Easter lamb roast? Well, if you are pally with farmers you might get some. Anyway Mum said that after her and Harriet's unannounced visits they would give us the cold shoulder - and not a shoulder of lamb, either. She can be funny you know!

Of course Auntie Betty couldn't resist having a go.

'And just now that we have an extra mouth to feed.'

Mind you, Ben is so small that he's not likely to eat a lot.

In the following months rationing extended to just about everything and would be going on much longer than anybody had expected. It also would have a profound and lasting effect on the way we thought and our attitude to food and waste.

In a way I didn't mind not having a full belly, as my heart was full...full of Remy. Planet Love was a lovely place to be, when jealousy didn't raise its ugly head. It was a place where you walked on pink clouds, everything went smoothly and everybody lived happily ever after including small, lonely children. And yet now and again reality intruded in my paradise and a hidden fear spoilt my joy. My father's letters, although heavily censored, hinted to troops departing for the continent and that meant that Remy might be going soon too. Truly, the more you love, the more you fear to lose. The war cast its shadow over our world and while I was happy to try to forget everything and live for the moment, I was aware that everything could soon change.

Weds 6 March

I have more company today. Batty Betty is complaining that Ben is getting under her feet while waiting to start school. Of course, the Harrigans didn't bother to send him. Anyway she has shoved him into the shop ordering him to make himself useful. Great. I'm stuck with him at night and during the day as well. Thank goodness he's starting to sleep better since I gave him my precious old teddy bear.

So today I was on the ladder reaching for an enormous tin of paint from the top shelf and Ben was holding the ladder for me at the bottom as the shop bell rang. I stepped down and nearly fell into two strong arms. Remy had come in and was holding the ladder for me. What a good excuse for a hug!

Ben stayed with me for a couple of days and indeed, he made himself useful. Small as he was, he was happy to climb up and down the ladder to get me stuff from the upper shelves. Of course I didn't let him handle money but he delighted in operating the cash register and hearing its 'ding'.

At home, Mum treated him with kindness, Auntie Betty tolerated him for the sake of the ration book and Robert's initial indifference had mellowed. In short, he was accepted by our family including Doug who, barring the occasional nip, seemed to have taken to him. Although still a nervous child, Ben was starting to relax but was strangely reluctant to talk about his family. We knew about the two women in his picture but there was no image of his father. Was there a father at all? And why did he lower his voice when he talked about Suzie?

Sun 10 March

Ben and my annoying brother have played together all day! Either Mum nagged Robert or he thought he should behave like the 'man of the house'.

Anyway, they threw the cricket ball back and forth to each other all morning in the garden. Unfortunately sometimes they would step on Doug who was chasing the ball as well. We could hear Auntie Betty shrieking in the background in defence of her mutt. I spied on them a little bit and, surprise, I heard Ben chatting.

'I wish I'd had a brother like you, instead of Suzie'.

'Funny name for a lad'

'No, silly, Suzie's my half-sister'.

'Lucky you, I have a whole one.'

Ben giggled at that and said 'yes but she's much nicer than Suzie.'

When they came in for elevenses, a small slice of bread spread with margarine (UGH!) Ben's cheeks were pink and so were Robert's.

All in all it has been a nice Sunday, except for the margarine, the shortage of meat and (for me) Remy's absence. But, as everybody including people on the wireless keeps saying 'Mustn't grumble.'

We were all aware that we had a new person in the house and, in our different ways we were trying to help him. He was shy and physically on the small side and there was something about him that worried me. It was as if he carried a shadow. But he was thrilled to be in Robert's company and looked at him with adoring eyes.

It slowly came out that Ben's relationship with his sister Suzie was not an easy one. She seemed to have little affection for the child and could treat him quite harshly, especially when out of their mother's sight. I couldn't understand how she could be so unfeeling. It is true that children can be cruel at times, but the Suzie in the picture was no longer a child. The father was still a mystery to us. When asked, Ben said he didn't remember him at all.

Mon 11 March

Tonight our 'bather' that horrid Sergeant Higgins turned up while Mum was away. We certainly weren't expecting him so late and Betty was rather put out. However, the smarmy fellow started buttering her up and she re-discovered her patriotic streak. Nothing was too much for our brave heroes, so she sent ME to give him clean towels. Urgh!

That hateful man started telling me what a nice girl I was and that I should stay away from common soldiers, not like that silly friend of mine... and all the way he was ogling me and trying to pat my cheek. What a creep!

Still, I am worried about Peg. She seems to be getting a reputation.

And so she was. Andrew, Remy's friend, had taken to boasting about his easy conquest. He was enjoying a little, uncomplicated affair with a not-too-shy country girl. Unfortunately, the not-too-shy girl had a big, romantic dream of love and marriage with a 'war hero' and Private Andrew Miller seemed to fit the bill.

My war hero had a different attitude. He didn't boast about what had passed between us, although we had not gone as far of course. As it happens, he was uncomfortable with Andrew's bragging and even more so with his continuous innuendos about us two. Their recent friendship was definitely cooling down.

Weds 13 March

Ben is at school now. He and a few lucky evacuees have been given places in Robert's posh college rather than in the village school. I wonder how he will cope with the snooty-nosed nobs who attend it. When my brother started there he had a few rough days but quickly won everybody over. Poor Ben however seems to be a natural target for bullying. We'll see.

I was concerned about Ben. I was becoming rather attached to the kid and from the little he let out about himself and his family it appeared he was a gentle, fragile child who had gone through quite a lot in his short life. I feared he would not fit into the new school and that he would be bullied but, as it turned out, I needn't have worried. Robert might have despised him at the beginning but had developed a rather proprietary attitude towards him. Ben was "our" evacuee and as such my brother felt entitled to protect him. Any attempt at bullying, and there were several, was quickly countered by Robert's sharp tongue and soon Ben was left alone, as were the other new kids.

Things hadn't gone so smoothly in the village school however and punch ups between the evacuees and the local pupils occurred often in the first few weeks. It took some time but eventually things settled and it must be said that air raid alarms helped in this respect. There is nothing that brings people together, in every sense, more than huddling and trying to comfort each other in the darkness of a shelter.

Sat 16 March

Last week the War Committee had the great idea of organising a football match to bring the evacuees and the community together. So today two mixed teams of evacuees and local children, the Hawks and the Eagles met and the Vicar offered to act as a referee. The Hawks wore a blue armband and the Eagles a red one. The match started and things started to go wrong. Arthur Stone of the Hawks fouled one of the evacuees of the Eagles and flattened him. The evacuee's brother, of the Eagles, turned on his teammate Arthur and punched him on the nose.

The whole match descended into chaos with some evacuees and locals fighting one another all over the pitch and the rest egging them on. The air was blue with swearwords but not as blue as the poor Vicar's face as he kept blowing his whistle but nobody took a blind bit of notice. And Cribbles was also ignored. His shrill voice was lost in the general mayhem and things calmed down only when some farmers intervened by pulling the kids apart and cuffing them soundly.

On the whole, I learned a number of interesting new words and also that it's definitely NOT true that sport brings people together.

If there was a thing Cribbles couldn't tolerate it was being overlooked. Such an affront, like during the football match, deserved a swift retribution. So the next day he was seen going around the village at dinnertime, nose up in the air. He was sniffing for evidence of unpatriotic Sunday roasts being eaten by people with little respect for meat rationing. If some mouth-watering aromas wafted towards his nostrils he would knock on people's door and demand to see what was in the pot. It must be said that it is not unusual for country people to keep chickens or to come across the odd rabbit. However, to Cribbles these were "unauthorised sources of meat" and therefore highly reprehensible. Well, he got some sharp answers this time. It is never a good idea to come between an Englishman and his roast, war or no war.

Mon 18 March

Today Remy popped briefly into the shop and said he had something for me. He just had the time to give me an envelope and off he went to re-join his unit that was passing through the village. In the envelope there was a picture of Remy with some of his comrades including Andrew. The nice thing was that above him there was a speech bubble with my name in it and a little heart like this

How sweet!

What was not quite so sweet was Peg's reaction when I showed it to her. 'It's alright for you' she said bitterly.

It seems that Andrew hasn't made an effort to see her and she was quite upset and, I'm afraid, a bit jealous about my continuing story with Remy.

A customer came in and put a stop to Peg and she walked away.

Poor Peg, she was really worried over Andrew's disappearance. Although he had been seen in the village, he hadn't bothered to look for her. I didn't fully appreciate the root cause of her anguish, nor did she yet, and I thought she was overdoing it. To be honest, between Remy, Ben and the shop I had less time for my friend.

She sensed it and the small spark of jealousy raised by my happier relationship with Remy started smouldering. Not only that, she had taken an immediate dislike to Ben and resented the time I had been spending with him.

Fri 22 March

Blast Betty! She has complained to the Hateful Higgins about Remy pestering me in the shop and that creep has promised to 'Keep that Frenchie in his place'. Not only that. He came up to me with his stupid smirk, called me a naughty girl and, as I turned away from him he put his dirty paw on my bottom. I turned on him like a viper and my face must have told him what I felt because he stepped away and muttered 'well, you like soldiers, don't you?'

Great, now I have a reputation too!

Auntie Betty's intervention gave fruit. In the following days Remy and to a point Andrew, could not move without being reprimanded and disciplined for all sorts of imaginary misbehaviours. They were regularly put on a charge and their visits to the village and the shop ceased. Remy in particular was mocked by Higgins about his 'smarmy French ways with a stupid girl' and assigned to latrine duties. His ironical and very French reply 'Oh merde!' earned him more of the same.

So, for a while, the only contact I had with Remy was the one bath he had at Mrs Bassett's. I went to try and see him in the garden and even then I fell under Betty's disapproving gaze and disparaging comments

'That Bassett woman encourages them'.

Peg had no such luck with Andrew. He never showed up. Private Miller had obviously enjoyed some country hanky-panky that did not mean much to him while it meant the whole world to her.

March 24 Easter

This morning we all went to church for the Easter service. We were wearing our best clothes but of course not new ones because of the war. This didn't seem to apply to Grace Cummings who was showing off in a new frock with a big lace collar. Quite a contrast to poor Peg who looked rather dowdy in an old mustard – coloured dress. However the service was nice and we all sang the hymns including Ben who was piping at the top of his voice. After that we went home to our tiny roast lamb dinner. Fortunately we had plenty of vegetables from the garden and mum had managed to rustle up an apple pie.

After lunch Robert, Ben and I went for a walk along the river and we were ordered by Betty to take Doug with us. The horrible mutt spotted a huge cow pat and promptly rolled in it. Imagine Betty's shrieks when we arrived home and she saw her precious pet covered in poo!

The worst of it was that we had to wash the creature in the bath before tea. So the bath has seen two animals now – Higgins and Doug.

At teatime Ben proudly showed us the eggs that Robert had helped him to paint and we ate them with a slice of bread. I was quite happy but suddenly the absence of Dad really hit me. I looked at Mum and saw that she had tears in her eyes. I reached for her hand and we didn't need to say anything.

Sat 30 March

Remy hasn't come for his weekly bath at Mrs Bassett's and is not around. I miss him so much. I miss his smile and his hand holding mine. I bet it's all Batty Betty and Hateful Higgins fault. Why can't they leave us alone, stupid interfering busybodies!

I feel like crying but I don't want to give Auntie Betty the satisfaction of seeing me so upset. And anyway today I was so busy in the shop that I didn't have the time even for a sniffle. It was so bad that Robert himself had to come down to lend a hand. My little brother is as sharp as a nail and understood that something was wrong. He didn't say anything but he had a rather worrying glint in his eyes.

Robert, despite his rather superior attitude, really cared for me and if he couldn't help me in my story with Remy at least would try his best to punish the evildoers.

If I was heartbroken at the prospect of seeing Remy only once a week, if at all, just imagine how Peg felt. Her Andrew, not one of the village's regular bathers, hadn't made any effort to see her and had just disappeared from the scene. Also, and this was much worse, he hadn't sent her any letters or messages, despite her efforts to contact him. Peg was devastated and her sad little face did not escape Robert's notice. Sergeant Higgins was out of his range, but Auntie Betty was a much easier prey and he prepared his trap.

He had a schoolmate write her a note, supposed to be from Mr Cribbles, and that was clever, as Auntie Betty was not familiar with Cribbles handwriting but knew Robert's well. The note, which was mysteriously delivered with the morning post (thanks, Billy!) dealt with the possible presence of an enemy spy in our midst and appealed to her patriotism to help discover it. Betty, as an outsider, would be not tied to any village loyalties and therefore able to conduct an impartial investigation. Cribbles swore her to secrecy and arranged to meet her in total privacy in a few days' time in the War Committee room half an hour before the Council ladies were due to arrive there. This was the aim of Robert's plan, to set up a secret meeting between Cribbles and Auntie Betty.

APRIL

Tues 2 April

Peg has spent the whole afternoon crying over my shoulder, between one customer and the next, because of Andrew's silence. I'm not exactly a bunch of laughter myself and I'm missing Remy like mad but at least I'm not so lachrymose (another of Robert's fancy words). Well, I suppose she has plenty of reasons to be so, with her mother on her back all the time, telling her not to make such a spectacle of herself.

However I think that Peg is far too clingy and that might have put Andrew off. That and, of course, Batty Betty's meddling.

And, talking about Auntie Betty, she is looking rather smug and also odder than usual. Her eyes seem to be darting in all directions and she has taken to whispering in Doug's ears. What on earth is going on?

The fake letter from Mr. Cribbles had its effect on Betty and she took her "mission" very seriously. She had always been one for snooping and now she could do it with a sense of pride. Unfortunately, she wasn't very subtle and people started to notice her odd behaviour. Also, whenever she came across Cribbles she would look at him intently and occasionally even winked at him, which probably disconcerted him. People started to suspect an interest on her part, to the point that some busybody customer asked me if there was a romance going on there.

Thurs 4 April

Today I had to laugh at nosey Mrs Stone and her suspicions. Fine, Auntie Betty is behaving strangely, but a romance? No way. And anyway I have had enough of doomed romances, including my own.

I'm sad and I desperately miss Remy but I can't and won't be a cry baby. In fact, I spend a lot of time trying to comfort Peg who is terribly upset by Andrew's behaviour.

Maybe this coming Saturday our soldier boys will re-appear together, Remy for his bath and Andrew for Peg.

The day of Betty's secret meeting came and Robert sprung his trap. She went to the room where the unsuspecting Mr. Cribbles was drafting the agenda for the War Committee meeting. As she entered and closed the door Robert, who had got hold of the key and was laying in waiting, silently locked it behind her. I don't know what passed between the two of them but, when later they tried to get out of the room, they found themselves trapped and no amount of effort could make the damn door open.

They both wanted to get out before anybody came, to avoid being found in a ridiculous situation and they tried their best. The upshot of it was when the Committee ladies arrived and unlocked the door with the key that Robert had thoughtfully put back in its place, they found both of them red in the face and somewhat dishevelled from their efforts to break the door down. Of course the ladies jumped to the wrong conclusions: some were scandalised, others giggled and Harriet Mandeville, eyes brimming with mischief, read the pair of them a playful lecture about misbehaving in almost holy precincts, just like they had been silly teenagers.

Only Cribbles' awe of Harriet prevented him from exploding and he said with as much dignity as he could muster 'It is not what it seems. I have the greatest respect for Miss Betty' while she just looked dumbstruck and managed to walk away as red as a beetroot. As for the meeting, it had to be adjourned as nobody could keep a straight face after what had happened.

Fri 5 April

I just cannot stop laughing. Last night Auntie Betty came home looking like thunder and shut herself in her room with Doug. This morning Mum told me and Robert, with a twinkle in her eye, what had happened at the War Committee meeting. The impish look on Robert's face said it all.

The clever little brat has stitched Betty up finely, not to mention Cribbles. I couldn't help thinking that Dad would have enjoyed it so! Of course Mum told Robert off but I bet she was secretly pleased. Me, I am quite proud of my little brother and I find it really sweet that he thought up all this plot for me and Peg.

After these events Auntie Betty laid low for a while and stopped being so meddlesome. However the damage was done, Remy was rarely seen in Millside and Andrew not at all, much to Peg's increasing despair.

If Auntie Betty was chastened by her misadventure, Mr. Cribbles became even more unpleasant as if trying to punish the whole village for his humiliation. He would bark at people for going around without their gas masks and was forever brandishing his government-issued notebook to jot down real or imaginary infringements to the new war rules. "Cribbles scribbles!" became the new codeword for imminent danger.

People also started to suspect that the spate of false air raid alarms that occurred in the next few weeks were down to his foul temper over the whole business and this unfortunately led to a degree of slackness in observing all the due precautions despite the continuing warning broadcasts from the wireless.

Sun 7 April

I am walking on pink clouds again!

This morning as we left church my heart missed a beat. Who was there but REMY with a big smile and a bunch of flowers for... Mrs Bassett! I was slightly taken aback and heard Grace snigger but then Remy turned and winked at me. You should've seen Grace's face!

Once at home, while Mum and Auntie Betty were preparing lunch, I sneaked into the garden. Remy was there, waiting for me on the other side of the fence. His smile and his kiss said everything, as did the single red rose that he had hidden in Mrs Bassett's bunch as a gift for me.

* * *

By the end of the afternoon the pink clouds have gone. Peg has turned up to get at me over the absence of Andrew as if I had anything to do with it!

As I lift a few fragile, dried petals from the pages of my diary, I still remember that moment of complete happiness. Only one moment though, as my mind went also immediately back to Peg. I asked Remy about Andrew and his face darkened. They had fallen out. He told me that Andrew had taken to refer to Peg as his "little country tart." That didn't go down well with Remy and they had a punch up which earned them both further punishment by a sniggering Sergeant Higgins.

I couldn't stay long in the garden but the joy of Remy's visit remained with me, a lovely secret hidden in my 16 year old heart. I dared not tell Peg what had passed between us as she would have been utterly devastated. I tried to suggest that Andrew had not been really interested in her and not worth crying over but all I got in reply was a brusque 'I thought you were my friend' as she turned her back and walked away from me.

Our friendship was breaking under the strain of her disappointment and to this day I regret it. We were growing apart at the very moment when she most needed a friend's help.

Weds 10 April

I'm quite upset about Peg. I know I'm luckier than her with my love story, but friends are supposed to share your joys as well as your sorrows. She's loaded me with her sorrows but cannot accept my joy. IT IS NOT FAIR!

Anyway today Hateful Higgins came back for his bath and I took good care to be out of his way. Not so Peg who went up to him trying to get some inkling about Andrew. Not a very good idea given Higgins' groping habit.

It definitely was not. Poor Peg. Higgins just looked at her in his smarmy way saying "Now, now young lady, you don't expect me to give away military secrets, do you?" With that he pretended to pat her shoulder in a semi-paternal way and let his hand stray on her boobs, the dirty pig!

Peg was still trembling as she told me this.

I really wanted to be there for Peg, to listen to her, to calm her down but at the same time I was afraid of letting her discharge all her pain on me. It is true that my story with Remy was a happier one but I also had other worries. I still missed my father very much. I missed his advice, his jokes and his calm good sense. At sixteen it is not easy to be managing a shop, a distraught friend, a stroppy aunt and a scared little boy.

I realise I sounded a bit drippy, but that is teenagers for you. In those times, at sixteen we were regarded as adults and lumbered with adults' duties while we were sometimes still children inside. I tried to be mature and carry my share of responsibilities and more, but at the same time I felt I could easily break under their weight.

Yet there was a stubborn streak inside me that allowed me to carry on. I would not be easily beaten.

Thurs 11 April

Today something quite extraordinary happened. A man and a girl got out of a dusty but smart car and, out of the blue, knocked on our door asking for Ben. He was still at school and so we invited them in. It turned out they were a flashy chap called Sid and Ben's sister Suzie. My, how striking she is!

Auntie Betty tutted in disapproval at her make up, showy clothes and jewellery but Robert and Ben who'd arrived in that moment were left staring – Robert in admiration and Ben in what looked like fear.

They had brought a parcel for Ben and Suzie handed it to him without even the hint of a hug. The man went "Allo nipper, aren't you pleased to see me" and made to muss his hair but Ben jumped back looking pale.

They didn't stay after that but left in a hurry. What an odd couple and what odd behaviour from Ben!

They were an odd couple indeed. He must have been about 15 years older than her and twice her size. A loud man with an easy smile and an overtly friendly attitude and yet there must have been some reason for Ben's reaction. I remember asking him while we were unpacking the clothes that Ben's mother had sent. All I could get was:

'Mum likes him but I don't.'

Did his Mum like him so much as to entrust him with Suzie? And what about the girl? She was dressed in a too grown-up way for her age and wore too much make up and showy trinkets. And to go round the country in a car with an older man was, and still is, more than a little improper, as Betty put it.

Sat 13 April

Of course the arrival of two strangers in a car has set tongues wagging. More than one customer has asked me about them wondering why this flashy pair had come to our house. 'Mind your own business' wasn't a possible reply, so I just said that they were visiting Ben.

Another tongue wagging has been Peg's. She'd caught a glimpse of the odd couple and couldn't stop talking about how lucky some girls are: beautiful, well dressed, and with a rich man in tow!

Unfortunately some more spiteful remarks about Suzie's appearance have been made and in Ben's hearing too. Grace Cummings hasn't held back. She has openly condemned Suzie's behaviour, looks and morals, just like Betty had done, and she wasn't even there! Not only that, on seeing Ben later on she put up her chin and snorted in disapproval. She looked like a blooming horse, I tell you!

Ben took all this to heart, even more so when the visit was talked about by the older village boys with a fair amount of sniggering. Every time the story was repeated, the details grew bigger, the car, the makeup, the jewellery. Ben instead seemed to shrink every time someone mentioned Suzie, which typically Betty did often. There is only so much a little boy can take.

Sun 14 April

What a fright! As we went into Church we heard a bit of sniggering over Suzie and Ben excused himself – we thought it was a call of nature but when he didn't reappear at the end of the service Mum sent Robert home to look for him. A bit later Robert came back running, all red in the face, saying Ben was nowhere to be found.

We all started looking round the village but no trace of him. Philip suggested it was time for an organised search party and naturally Cribbles got busy. Some people were sent off to the Farmers' Hall, others to Albany Court school and even to the Manor House. Harriet Mandeville drove around the country lanes, hoping to spot him while myself, Robert, Philip and, would you believe it, Doug headed to the old water mill.

At one point Doug was straining on his leash and we knew we were on the right track, so we let him go. We followed him to the mill and searched and called but no response, yet Doug was running around and yapping and that must've meant something. Then he started sniffing by the water wheel and as we reached the edge of the millpond we saw a boy's cap floating on the water. My heart sank and I screamed 'Ben'.

We did find him but in what a state! He barely answered my call. He'd managed to wedge himself between the wheel and the wall as if he wanted to disappear. Philip waded in and got him out. Wet, cold and miserable but alive. Robert wrapped him in his Sunday blue jacket, Philip carried the little boy back and the search was called off.

I remember my sense of relief, the gratitude for the people who helped in the search and my bitterness towards those who considered the whole incident like an unwelcome intrusion into their Sunday routine. Also, and I am really sorry to say that, I remember my astonishment at Peg's reaction. Not only did she refuse to join the search but when we came back with Ben, she berated me for forgetting that we had planned to spend the afternoon together.

'You care more for this little brat than me,' she said. And you know what? From that moment I did and turned my back on her.

Weds 17 April

I haven't had time to write because guess what. DAD HAS BEEN AT HOME on leave for 3 days since Sunday night. It was a complete surprise and Mum nearly swooned when she saw him! He lifted her in his arms and twirled her around and did the same with me. He almost approached Auntie Betty but she froze him with a glare. Never mind.

He hugged Robert and spotted Ben trying to hide behind him.

'So this is our little guest' he said and made to pat him on the head but Ben pulled back.

He came to the shop and checked things and complimented me on my running of the business and Mum on her bookkeeping.

We didn't have all of Dad for 3 days as he went around the village calling on friends and stopped in the pub, but we loved every minute he spent with us. Just imagine: swotty Robert bunked off school!

Dad told us funny stories about his life in the Army but was reluctant to say anything of real importance. The slogan "Careless talk costs lives" was pasted everywhere and military men knew this better than anybody. However, he hinted that things were heating up abroad and that he would be off very soon. 'Oh God' I thought. Dad… and Remy.

Fri 19 April

Today the whole village prepared to celebrate St George's Day, 3 days early. After lessons, the children were dressed up in unstitched pillowcases painted with a red cross, made to look like tabards.

Being the Vicar's children, Philip and Grace were given the leading parts even if they are now too old for it. Also a sheet was painted green ready to be draped on an old donkey to make it look like a dragon. Another example of make do. I can't wait to see the final result.

We usually didn't make such a fuss about St George's Day but we were at war and we were expected to be as patriotic as possible, as Cribbles put it. This seemed to be the perfect occasion for a display of English pride, as well as having a bit of fun, as the war was grinding us down. It would also be an occasion to bring people together and to heal the little rifts created by the gossiping flying around after all the recent events.

Sun 21 April.

To celebrate St George's day we all gathered on the village green. The children in their tabards were armed with wooden sticks pretending to be swords. An embarrassed-looking Philip, as Saint George, was leading his troops and Grace, all draped in white, was looking smug, as the Princess.

But instead of fighting the 'dragon' the children start whacking one another. And soon the old division reappeared, locals against evacuees with Philip and Grace stuck in the middle.

Cribbles tried to keep some sort of order shouting that the enemy was the dragon and how can you win a war if you fight among yourselves. But nobody listened. I almost felt sorry for him and I thought he had a point for once.

More than everything, I felt sorry for Philip who had been forced into this pageant almost against his will, but I had no sympathy for Grace who never lost a chance to act the primadonna. As for Cribbles, he hated not being in control of an event he himself had helped to promote and so he used the only means at his disposal to re-assert his authority. He set off the air raid siren. This sent everybody scuttling for shelter but when no airplanes appeared in the sky, we finally put two and two together: Cribbles was the only person to have access to the siren. How could we take the alarms seriously after that?

Tues 23 April

Today I got a glimpse of Remy as he was passing through the village in a staff car, I was standing in the shop's door and he winked and waved at me with a big smile. More army lorries followed. There is something definitely going on and on the wireless there is news of our troops in action abroad. I am SO worried about Remy leaving.

I remember wondering whether I would see Remy again now that the war had passed its 'phoney' phase. For the first time my fear about Remy's safety overcame my fear for my father's. Of course I knew that Dad was equal to anything and yet I felt I was being disloyal.

For me, as for many people, the war was a necessary evil to stop the greater evil of the Nazi threat but for my father it was a duty and for young, spirited soldiers it was an adventure.

For Remy it was more than that, it was a mission to help France. In fact, despite his love for me, he was impatient to go. All the interminable drills on the parade ground got under his skin and he could not wait to see the last of Sergeant Higgins and his sneering face.

Thurs 25 April

This morning the wireless announced that, to support the war effort, taxes were going up and also the price of stamps, so Auntie Betty immediately sent Ben to buy a whole load of them.

He came back looking very hangdog and with only 6 stamps, earning a scolding from Betty. He was on the point of bursting into tears so she relented and asked him what was the matter. It turned out that at the Post Office Peg, who was helping her Mum to cope with an unexpected queue, had shouted at him in front of everybody. 'You lot want everything.' Ben couldn't understand the outburst and kept saying that she was just like Suzie.

Deep down I know that Peg is thinking of me and Remy, I have my love while she.... Well, one small consolation: she sees Ben as part of our family.

Just as well, because it was clear to us that Ben's family life was not a happy one. He had a difficult relationship with his older sister and his mother, apart from sending him some clothes, had not been in contact with him. As for his father, we had learned that he had died shortly after Ben's birth. Maybe this had something to do with the two women's behaviour towards the boy. I was starting to learn that when people are unhappy they lash out and look for somebody to blame. In a way Peg was a prime example of that.

Sun 28 April

I am in Heaven. Well, I was.

This morning as we left church who was waiting for me outside?

YES, REMY!

He came towards us, introduced himself and asked Mum whether he could take me for a walk. Mum beamed at him (I wonder whether she's had a chat with Mrs Bassett) and Robert smirked. Betty however stated that I would go nowhere without a chaperone and sent Ben to fetch Doug. She must think I need a dog to guard over my virtue.

All this was a little embarrassing as it happened in front of everybody but, hey, Grace's face was worth the embarrassment.

I felt SO happy but then I caught sight of Peg. She was looking at me with pure hatred.

This page was torn and the rest was missing but I remembered everything.

We were almost a proper married couple as we strolled off with a kid and a dog. The air was fresh, the grass was green and Remy was so handsome. I tottered holding on to his arm in a state of bliss (Mum had lent me a pair of her high heels, not very suitable for a country ramble). It was 20 years ago yet I remember clearly walking along the canal and thinking life would stay like this forever. Even the overhead drone of one of our RAF boys in his Spitfire could not bring me back down to earth.

At the start of the year I had lost my father to the Army but now I had two new men in my life. The older one was holding my arm and the younger one had run ahead with Doug who seemed on his best canine behaviour. Ben's shoes were down at heel and scuffed, his socks sagged around his ankles but his skinny legs carried him running happily after his new four-legged friend.

Remy spotted a bench under a weeping willow and guided me over to it putting his arms around my waist. He then bent to kiss me, a long, tender kiss that lasted until we heard a rasping shout. 'So, this is what you are up to now, Miss goody-two-shoes.'

Peg stood before us, hair in a mess, cheeks red from catching us up, her prim, dowdy Sunday best at odds with her wild appearance.

I gasped but Remy coolly asked why she had followed us.

'I want to be with my man too' she almost shouted.

'Do you mean Andrew?'

'Of course' she shrieked "Do you think there have been that many?"

'Peg, Peg, don't you think he would have been in touch if he was really interested?' I said trying to make her see reason.

But Peg was far too gone to listen.

'So, you too are against me now, but I'll show you!' and with that she turned and stomped along the canal.

Ben had stood back while this ugly scene was playing itself out, looking white-faced and scared. There was no sign of the dog. Peg spotted the boy and told him to scram but he just stood still.

The sound of the air raid siren wailed overhead. Remy told me to look after Ben while he ran after Peg, bringing her back to stand with us in our natural shelter. I will never forget her look of loathing and exhaustion, as she was clutching her stomach, slumped onto the seat. Finally the air raid alarm stopped and there was a silence in the air and among us that lasted until the dog's bark from up the canal broke it.

Remy then walked us back to the village and left.

When Ben and I got home we were met by my family's anxious faces. Their worry over me and Ben and my own upset over Peg made for a very quiet Sunday.

MAY

Fri 3 May

Today Gorgeous George left for the Army, and what a send off it was!

He was followed by a group of young people, mostly girls who noisily waved him goodbye, as he mounted on his motorcycle. Cribbles was there as well, terribly miffed because the speech he had prepared to salute our young hero was drowned among the cheers and the shouts of good luck.

I had briefly closed the shop to be there and was surprised not to see Peg among the other girls. It isn't like her to miss such an occasion.

I later learned that Peg had, in fact, other plans. In her desperation she "ambushed" George outside the village and asked for a lift to the Regiment's headquarters. He good naturedly agreed and rode with her all the way there. He then left for the recruiting centre while Peg started to make enquiries about Andrew.

The sight of a rather dishevelled, anxious girl asking after a soldier raised a few eyebrows, among the officers. Unfortunately, it also raised some sniggering, wolf whistles and dubious offers of assistance among the soldiers. Poor Peg got more and more upset and burst into a flood of tears.

Luckily an angel, in the shape of Harriet Mandeville, came to her rescue. She had been at lunch with the garrison's commander and was on her way to her car. On hearing the commotion, she had turned and seen Peg surrounded by laughing soldiers. Quickly Harriet had pushed her way to Peg's side, taken her arm and guided her towards her car. It says much for Harriet's good sense and good nature that she refrained from telling Peg off or from asking her probing questions. On the way back to Millside Peg started to open up and to tell Harriet about some of her woes and problems. Only some though. The biggest was still unknown, even to herself.

Sun 5 May

Today Peg and her family weren't in church. I know Peg's got the hump but the whole lot of them? As per usual Mr Harrigan had something spiteful to say about people being too lazy to go to church. Harriet Mandeville overheard him and froze him by answering that some people are too mean and quick to pass judgement. That put a stop to any other gossip but people are still wondering about them.

As far Auntie Betty, she had no doubts. 'That Peg is going a bad way' she said, and turning to Ben 'Just like that sister of yours'. The poor boy flinched and hung his head. The fact is Betty said that in Mrs Bassett's hearing and got her comeuppance.

'For shame, Betty Jones, you have been the subject of gossip yourself.' That shut Betty up and for the rest of the day she took pains to be nice to Ben.

Weds 8 May

This is SO strange; the Post Office is still closed, Peg and her family are not around and the red van has disappeared. Good neighbours have knocked on the Fletchers' door and not received any answers. In short they've gone away without telling anybody and rumours are spreading like wildfire.

The ever-nosy Mrs Stone has come to the shop to ask me what's going on with Peg and family. As if I'd tell her anything!

Yes, the whole village was wondering about the mystery and looking for explanations. There were a few jokes about Widow Fletcher running away with the post office till, but most people were starting to comment about Peg's recent odd look and odder behaviour.

The only person who knew what was going on was keeping mum. When taking Peg home after her escapade, Harriet had stopped for a talk with Mrs. Fletcher. Harriet was a woman of the world and it had not taken her long to guess Peg's condition. A stunned Mrs. Fletcher was persuaded to make contact with a relative of hers in another county that would take care of an errant girl - without any scandal.

Fri 10 May

The mystery is solved and the cat is out of the bag. Mrs Stone told me in the shop, rather smugly, that everything was now clear. She had it from her husband that the Fletchers' disappearance was being talked about in the pub and who walks in but Sergeant Higgins. Of course he knew what had been going on and lost no time in telling everybody about the scene at the barracks and commenting on Peg's state. 'I know what a bun in the oven looks like' he said. I wonder if he'd caused a few of them, seeing his behaviour towards women.

'No mystery about the father either' he said and I bet a lot of the customers remembered Private Miller.

So, this is it. Peg, oh Peg! Poor Peg!

Poor Peg indeed. Pregnant, abandoned, exiled. What a big price to pay for a single mistake. In a way, she too was a victim of the war.

Sat 11 May

Mum came in from the War Committee meeting INCANDESCENT. The ladies were passing comments on Peg's disgrace and sniping 'these girls that go out with soldiers' clearly meaning ME as well. The vicar's wife was even more direct and went on to Mum about the standards of behaviour expected from young ladies. Mum was about to explode when Harriet Mandeville stepped in. 'Not all girls and all soldiers are the same.' And that settled the matter.

It may have settled the matter there, but not for me. I'm angry with them, angry with the whole village and, I must admit, also angry with poor Peg.

That was village life for you. Yes, our village gave us a sense of safety and of belonging but it also caged and trapped us in its narrow society and narrower outlook. Within its confines there was little scope to be really ourselves. Either you stuck to its time-honoured ways or you were ostracised. It could be a hotbed of gossip where everything and everybody was discussed, dissected and often condemned. Fortunately, there were a few open-minded people that were able to see that times were changing and we needed to change with them.

Sun 12 May

I'm still smouldering so much that I haven't gone to church, not to see the smug looks of Grace and her mother. Mum put a brave face on and went with Robert and a reluctant Betty who really wanted to stay at home and keep an eye on me. Great now I'm to be under guard. Ben wanted to stay to keep me company but I told him to go.

I need time to myself, I need time to think. I'm still surprised at my own reaction towards Peg. How could I possibly be angry with her, and yet...

I can now understand why Peg has been so nasty towards me as if it was all my fault. Yes, she did what she did in my shop but after all that was her choice.

I felt then that my friendship with Peg had ended and I wouldn't have anything to do with her anymore. And though I didn't realise it at the time, Peg's dig that I had been Miss Goody Two Shoes had hurt.

I also had to accept that I had been the one to turn a blind eye to her using the storeroom in the shop to fool around with Andrew. But, like her, I was only 16 and although I had the responsibilities of an adult, an adult I was not. And of course, I was in love.

Tues 14 May.

We are still all buzzing from yesterday's speech on the wireless by Churchill

'We shall fight them on the beaches, we shall fight on the landing grounds, we shall fight in the fields...' and I shall fight them from behind the shop counter. I don't mean only the Germans, but also the village gossips and Auntie Betty.

However, who got the greatest buzz of all was Cribbles who has appointed himself leader of the newly-created Home Guard. Apparently our oldies are going to be enlisted to defend us all in case of a German invasion. Pity that they are the first to scuttle for cover when they hear the drone of an aircraft overhead.

So yesterday's big speech completely overshadowed the return of the post office van with the Fletchers minus Peg. Where is she? What happened to her?

At that stage I didn't know where Peg was, so I decided to ask Billy. He looked mysterious but I knew that he was sweet on me and it did not take me long to get the whole story out of him. Peg wouldn't be coming back.

I remember feeling so stupid and so bad about it all.

Thurs 16 May

Today there were two lovely surprises and one ... Aunty Betty.

The first surprise was a letter from Dad, once again heavily censored, with a picture of him and his mates in a strange village. I wondered where he is.

The second surprise was a visit from Remy who knocked on the shop window as I was checking the anti-shatter tape. I pulled him into the shop, I hadn't seen him for over two weeks. We kissed and I melted. I showed him Dad's picture and he recognised the setting. Dad was in France. Remy told me not to worry. In France you eat well.

We were about to kiss again when Batty Betty stormed into the shop and literally chased Remy away. 'One girl already got ruined, you are not going to ruin this one,' she shouted red in the face. And Remy had to back off and leave. Thank you Betty!

I was really miffed but my love was not to be daunted so easily. He was no coward, but he understood Betty's concern. Peg's name had circulated freely among the troops, thanks to Andrew Miller and Sergeant Higgins. Remy realised how easily a reputation could be ruined. He was however still determined to see me and knew exactly what to do: he went to Mrs Bassett's.

Besides being always very nice to him, she had another advantage - an alleyway that ran beside her garden and ours.

Sat 18 May

I'm still annoyed at Betty's meddling. What is particularly bad is that since Thursday she has been popping into the shop every few minutes looking around to check that Remy hasn't snuck back. She's strutting around very pleased with herself and getting in the way of the customers.

Not that we have many, as the old codgers have been rounded up and forced to undergo military training. They have just paraded past the shop in a collection of old work clothes as they wait for their uniforms. Any 'martial air' has been spoilt by a tail of scruffy kids that followed them pretending to march, proudly carrying sticks for guns, Ben and Doug among them. At least they made me laugh.

The Home Guard looked a bit comical but they took themselves very seriously. In fact all kinds of people were called to support the war effort and they generally showed commitment, if not always enthusiasm.

Even Robert's posh school organised its own cadet unit and my brother started to attend military training sessions every day for one hour after school and two hours on a Saturday morning.

Of course, this made him too tired to be of any help in the shop.

Sun 19 May

Sunday and church again. And again, Grace's smug face when she took me aside and asked me about my soldier beau.

'You must be disappointed just like your silly friend' she said. 'But then nice girls don't go with common soldiers'.

'I don't see any nice girls here, just snidey little bitches' I said and walked away.

Fact is that Betty has been boasting about sending Remy on his way to protect my good name and Grace has got wind of it.

So she's having a go at me even though she had an interest in him herself. The little hypocrite.

Thurs 23 May

It's nearly midnight and I cannot sleep. Ben is snoring softly in his bed and I'm still up thinking of Remy. This afternoon we had another air raid alarm and although it came to nothing, as per usual, it brought back the war. My Dad is fighting in France and soon Remy might be there as well.

What is this noise from the garden?

Someone was tapping on my window. I stopped writing, went to the window and I saw Remy. Very quietly I went to the back door and fell into his arms. When he released me, I noticed he looked grave and his usual cheery smile wasn't there. He said he had left the barracks without permission to come and see me as the next day he would be on his way to France. My world fell apart. We could not stand there risking being overheard, so we made for the Anderson shelter. It was as if this horrible space has suddenly transformed into a cosy, romantic refuge for two lovers soon to be parted. I know, this sounds too much Romeo and Juliet, but this is how we felt and, just like Shakespeare's couple we had our first night together. Never mind the damp, never mind the smell, what really counted were our bodies.

We were still nesting in each other's arms when the air raid siren sounded. As it happened, we were in the right place. So, we quickly tidied ourselves up and tried to look respectable although we knew we would have some explaining to do when the rest of the family and Ben joined us.

Suddenly a loud blast rocked the shelter, followed by the sound of smaller explosions. We heard screams and cries and as I made for the shelter door desperate to find my family, Remy held me back. It wasn't safe to be outside, so we stayed put for a little while, unaware of the drama in the house. Then we came out and went down the alleyway hoping not to be noticed.

The bomb was a direct hit on the shop. The front of the house had caved in and the small explosions were the tins of paint bursting into flames and scattering pieces of metal everywhere. The staircase had partially collapsed leaving just about enough steps for my family to get out. My mother wrapped in an old dressing gown and with her hair singed was desperately looking everywhere for me. A shaken Betty clutching Doug was supported by Robert but somebody was missing.

The neighbours already starting to gather on the pavement were suddenly pushed aside by Cribbles. In his role as Air Warden and supported by four of his Home Guard he took command of the situation and tried to make everybody move away because of the danger of collapse. Cries were heard from the rubble and my mother screamed hysterically but at that moment I came out from the alleyway, while Remy stood back. Mum grabbed me, calling my name over and over again and only after asked 'Where is Ben?'

I looked around in the flickering light of the burning paint tins and wreckage but couldn't see his little face. Just then his voice called out a feeble 'Annie...' from under the ruin of what had been the basement. I stepped towards it but Cribbles barred my way,

'The conditions of this property are unsafe according to regulation 538. No access is allowed. I am not having my Health and Safety record ruined.'

I shouted at him 'There's a child down there' but he wouldn't move. Mum, Robert and even Betty tried to talk Cribbles round but he stood his ground only flinching when Betty, the respectable, righteous, dutiful Betty called him a heartless bastard. His men also stood in rank against the villagers who were clamouring to save Ben, whose voice was getting weaker and weaker. But Cribbles wouldn't budge.

Suddenly, two strong arms lifted him out of the way. My love had stepped out of the dark alley determined to rescue Ben. Remy's uniform gave him a status in the eyes of the Home Guard and they made no attempt to stop him as he jumped into remains of our home. Some of the villagers, led by Philip, rushed to follow him, not caring about the danger and started to look for the little boy that had by now stopped calling. They doused fires and shifted beams but they couldn't find him until Doug started to scratch near a pile of rubble. He was laying there pinned down by a collapsed wall but when they reached him my Ben had stopped breathing.

Remy climbed up out of the smouldering building with Ben in his arms and came towards me, 'I am so sorry Annie, there is nothing more that I can do', and I understood.

He laid the body on an improvised stretcher and we all gathered around our little evacuee, crying. At that moment an ominous crack was heard from inside the timbers and the crowd pulled back as the rest of the house collapsed.

Remy used this moment to slip away unseen. Duty called and he knew he had to go back to the barracks before dawn. We were distraught, we had lost everything – house, shop, possessions. However, to me that mattered less than the loss of a shy little blond child.

Afterwards we all decamped to the Rectory, Ben was laid in the vestry and we tried to get some sleep, wrapping ourselves in borrowed blankets. The next three days passed in a blur of frantic activity. There was a telegram to be sent to Ben's family and to the Evacuation Office, legal paperwork to be sorted and accommodation to be found for us. There were also two more bombed sites to be inspected – a cow shed and the Farmer's Hall which had been hit in the same night.

We tried to salvage something from the ruins of our house and the whole village came to our rescue with offers of clothes, bedding and food. As per usual Mrs Bassett came up trumps – she opened her house to us and we went to stay with her. All except one – Robert got offered a full boarding place at his posh school.

Monday came, the day of Ben's funeral, a rather hurried affair. We hadn't heard from Ben's mother and we waited the whole morning but nobody showed up. So, after a quick service, the poor boy was put into the ground with only us and a few villagers there, his personal tragedy soon forgotten in the greater tragedy of war. Forgotten by everybody but not by me.

* * *

My diary ended there and I never kept another one again. As I was still musing over it a voice called out 'Quick! It's starting' and I braced myself to go to the cemetery. There, in front of the cameras, the press and the gathered villagers Suzie Bell was in full performance, smiling but with a touch of sadness. Her pretty head was covered with a dark mane, mainly chestnut but with a flash of red in the spring sunshine. She gave a short speech, reminiscing about her poor, sweet, little brother and graciously unveiled a marble headstone with bronze lettering. Then the vicar, old Mr Cummings introduced some of the villagers, me included. Suzie Bell shook hands with everybody but I pulled back and she pretended not to notice.

Hand-shaking over, she approached me.

'We can't just stay here by this stupid memorial glaring at each other' she hissed.

'There's a tea-room round the corner' I replied quietly.

'Oh, where the old ladies are sitting moaning and smelling of mothballs? Ain't exactly Leicester Square' said Suzie in an affected Cockney accent.

'We could probably sit in Mrs. Bassett's parlour, she'd understand.'

'You are full of understanding, aren't you?' sneered Suzie.

So here we were drinking Mrs Basset's tea, me and Suzie Bell looking so very pretty and with such a grand air. Her eyes wandered about the room as if inspecting it. An actress, I thought, she needs a set as well as an audience.

'The vicar told me how kind you were to my little brother' Suzie started.

'And he told me how unkind you were to him, downright cruel. And don't come here pretending to be sorry when you never bothered about him, you never loved him.'

She made a show of appearing indignant but realising I wasn't impressed changed tactics and replied softly.

'It's easy for you to have a go, you don't know the whole story.'

'Fine so tell me...' and everything came out.

Suzie's early years had been happy enough but the death of her mother when she was 9 had been a blow from which she had never recovered. The quick marriage of her father to Edith, a colleague at work, took her and everybody else completely by surprise and set tongues wagging, as did the appearance a few months later of a baby brother.

'Can you imagine that? My mother had not been in the ground six months and already he had replaced her with that...tart! And got her pregnant.'

Suddenly Suzie found herself having to share her father's attention with a stepmother and a squalling infant. Her father's delight with his new-born son rankled with Suzie and she took a dislike to the boy. As for the stepmother she was so preoccupied with the baby she simply had no time to spare for Suzie.

'I know all about that, I have a younger brother myself. But how could blame Ben, it was your parents' fault' I spat.

'Try to explain that to a 9 year old.'

Suzie's story was that they were now a family unit that excluded and rejected her, so she would pay them back in the only way she knew, she would reject THEM, starting with the little intruder. From that moment on a sullen Suzie ignored the little one, never picking him up when he cried, never responding to his gurgles and smiles, never helping out despite the scoldings and occasional slap that her mutinous attitude earned her.

'It was as if I forbade myself to love him' she said dramatically twisting her hands as if a camera was on.

That really set me up. Even then she could not stop playacting. Still, as she was opening up, I could see how difficult it must have been to maintain, or pretend to maintain, such an emotional distance from such a sweet little boy. However, I refused to feel sorry for her.

Suzie's voice was slightly husky as she continued with her tale. The sudden death of her father about one year later made matters much worse. She was locked in a battle of wills with her stepmother, with Ben caught in the middle. The woman, while not loving the girl, was determined to do her duty by her and tried her best to raise her properly, as Suzie herself acknowledged.

'Well' I said 'It seems to me she really failed in that job! At least she tried but did you try to be nicer to her and Ben?'

'I think we just about tolerated one another, as for Ben, it's fairly impossible to ignore a toddler, they are forever getting under your feet.' Suzie had somewhat relented towards him and she would occasionally play with him, but not for long and she would suddenly send him away, sometimes even with a clip around the earhole. To make up for this Edith then bought him a dog that became his main companion.

There was just a hint of defiance as she went on talking about herself growing up. Apparently, the Suzie at home was very different from the Suzie at school. There she allowed herself to show her true face: a gregarious, smart girl who could be very charming and even co-operative, if a little wilful. Suzie was pretty and had a sharpish tongue. She quickly made friends and gathered a small gang around her but, in a way, all her friends were a little afraid of her. There was a daredevil quality about her and she went further than any of the others, who were slightly older. When it came to boys, 13 year old Suzie was aware that she had no problems in attracting their attentions, wanted or otherwise. She was already filling a 32 inch bra and even the male teachers' glances stopped on her feminine figure. It was as if members of the opposite sex sniffed her out.

As she said this Suzie raised her head, flicked her hair and looked around, as if asking for approval or applause. I'm not narrow-minded but I must admit I was shocked by this open acknowledgment of her sexual allure. However, I could see the risk in all that. She couldn't have been mature enough to keep clear of predatory males.

'It must not be that easy to handle those situations at thirteen.' I grudgingly admitted.

'No, especially when you meet scheming men.'

Edith's widow pension was not enough to support the family, so she took in lodgers to make ends meet. Sometimes they tried it on, however they were people that came and went without having any real impact on Suzie's life, until Sid appeared.

'Who, that flashy man you showed up with?'

'Well, he wasn't that flashy then.'

He had arrived at their bungalow in Brighton wearing a suit that had seen better days, a rather loud tie and a slightly battered hat at a rakish angle on his head. No common cloth cap for him! Sid, at 28, was the kind of man who could worm his way in when it came to women, with a wink and a smile. When it came to men, they found his easy ways amusing but, as the saying goes, they would never have invited him into their club.

Suzie remembered the immediate change in the household with this new male presence. Edith began to pay more attention to her hair and make-up. Coming home from school Suzie would often find Edith and Sid chatting. Sid would have an arm around Edith's shoulders and Suzie felt she was in the way. He did not seem to keep regular hours although a regular trip to the pub with Edith was on the agenda. And while he was able to charm her stepmother, Suzie recalled that he chatted to her also from the start and would sometimes hug and pat her.

'What about Ben?' I asked.

'He did not have much time for Ben but he could be casually kind to him.'

He would on occasion take the two of them down to the seafront for an ice-cream. They would go in a scruffy white van which he used to transport props for his freelance work in Brighton's film studios and which he freely borrowed.

Suzie Bell continued with her story and I was interested to hear how she had managed to get a foot in the world of cinema. From her account it seemed to link to Sid. This character, as she put it, was quite adept at "borrowing" props left unclaimed after filming and storing them in his lock-up, a sort of Aladdin's cave full of tawdry fake treasures. He would pass these on in exchange for dodgy tobacco or alcohol, which he then sold to the film crew and occasionally also to some of the second-rate actors who rubbed shoulders with the gaffers in the pub. He had an eye for opportunities as well as an eye for pretty girls and saw the potential in Suzie, now a teenager.

'If not my talent, my tits' she sniggered. Well!

Sid would take her and Ben to the studios as a treat and was very happy to introduce her to some of the men there, and then making himself scarce with the excuse of looking after the boy.

I stared at her: 'Did they ask you how old you were?'

'Of course not' spat Suzie pouting a little. She had soon realised that it was her job to be "nice" to these gentlemen, with the understanding that she may get a part in a film.

'Talk about a girl at risk' I thought, although she was not exactly a lamb among wolves.

Once Suzie got in her stride, I could see the actress in her wouldn't let go. She was clearly playing for effect and enjoying it. Some of what she said was a bit much, however. I could have done without the graphic description of her success in tempting movie men with Sid's encouragement.

'Didn't you think it odd that older men were interested in you? Wasn't it just for one thing?' I asked pointedly.

'It was my chance to get into the movies'.

'Well, yes, I can see that. But using Ben as a cover for your encounters was wrong.'

Suzie smirked 'You don't say...the little so and so caused the worst row Edith and I ever had'. She seemed to miss the point I was making, or pretended to.

It came out that on one of these outings Ben had seen a cameraman being rather intimate with Suzie and later had innocently talked about her getting lots of cuddles in the full hearing of Edith.

'She screamed at me as soon as she understood what the little blighter was saying. We both let rip and I told her she was jealous because Sid preferred me to her. That really hit home although she went on and on about respectability.'

They were still at each others' throats when Sid walked in, coolly assessed the situation and set down to calm Edith. Suzie, he said, was going to earn good money and make a name for herself. Edith would benefit from that and finally get all the little luxuries she so deserved and be the beautiful lady she was meant to be.

Oh, Sid knew how to flatter Edith, to appeal to her interest and to her secret vanity. If flattery was his main weapon when dealing with problems, menace was the other. He whispered something to Ben that made the little boy blanch and mussed his hair as he used to do. Only, this time Ben yelped.

'What a cad!' I thought. 'And what a bitch!' Through gritted teeth I asked: 'How could you just stand there while he mistreated your little brother?'

'Bah, that was not real mistreatment. Anyway, I was angry with Ben myself. Although I must say that I felt a little sorry for him when he later came to ask me to tell Sid not to cut his tongue off. I told him not to be silly and that Sid was joking'.

But Ben must have been really scared, he was only 6 after all. From that moment on he tried to avoid Sid and would take himself to bed when he came home in the evening.

'The kid just went into his shell, he hardly spoke and stayed away from me as well.'

While the little boy drew more into himself, Suzie took her chance. Ben didn't come to the studio anymore, so she was able to concentrate on charming the crews under Sid's controlling eye. She had a lucky break when the casting manager took an interest in her, took her out, and gave her a small part in the latest production. She appeared at the right time in the run-up to the rise of wartime weepies and started to be cast in films which featured dramatic storylines. Suzie's pretty face fitted in to this type of production which always had a happy ending, garlanded with roses and a cottage door. She had changed her name from a rather ponderous Bellingham into the snappier Bell and Suzie Bell had the right ring, she said with a self-satisfied smile.

'Then you were already in the movies when you came to visit Ben? I didn't recognise you.'

My comment got a rather snooty reply.

'I am not surprised, I am sure you didn't get to see many pictures in this backwater.'

'This backwater had better things to do' I replied miffed.

Suzie Bell shrugged her shoulders and started to talk about all the upheavals in Brighton. At the beginning of the war the city had been declared a "safe place". so hundreds of evacuee children from all over Britain had been sent there. But soon after, the Military Intelligence revealed a possible imminent German invasion. The evacuation plan had to be reversed and all the youngsters including the locals, were quickly assembled, loaded on trains and trucks and scattered around the country at random, a bewildered Ben among them. Suzie, by then old enough not to be included, hadn't bothered to say good-bye to him before he was whisked off to Millside and she to her film set.

'Yes, as soon as I saw him at the Farmers' Hall, I saw how lost he looked' I said 'When he came to stay with us I really didn't know what to make of the poor little boy. He seemed fragile, both physically and emotionally. To start with he hardly spoke and we wondered what his family life was like.'

'It was a bed of roses' Suzie replied ironically.

I turned on Suzie 'You are making a joke of it but when you arrived with Sid, out of the blue, I saw Ben's fear. He went white. And you seemed not to care about him, Suzie. You almost threw his bag of extra clothes at him. And went away without looking back.'

'There wasn't much to look at, your sour faces in that dump of a house.'

'Maybe we had sour faces, maybe our house was a dump but at least there was some love in it and Ben felt it'.

For once, the actress was unable to raise to the occasion and just shrugged her shoulders.

I continued 'We all read Edith's letter around the kitchen table at home to try to see if we could make sense of Ben's background. It was then I began to realise my own little family wasn't so bad after all, even with Auntie Betty badgering everyone.'

Suzie smiled in that superior way of hers and that set my back up again.

'You were so focused on your career, so caught up in that whirlwind that you really didn't have time for your brother. I can sort of understand it. But MY GOD, both you and your mother missing the little one's funeral? How heartless is that!' I lashed out.

And it seemed to me that at those words a tear trembled in the corner of Suzie's eye. She certainly looked downcast as she said

'It looks bad, doesn't it.'

And then, raising her head.

'It was not for the lack of trying. I had returned to Brighton by then and, believe it or not I was devastated at the news.'

She shot me a challenging look and continued.

'Edith was in hysterics and I had to hold myself together to help her. But it was as if all the feelings I had kept locked inside me were clamouring to burst out and yet I couldn't let them. I asked Sid to take us to the funeral but it was impossible.'

Brighton had been cordoned off as the German invasion was expected any moment. The beachfront was strewn with barbed wire, there were roadblocks everywhere and there was a curfew. Private cars were not allowed on the roads and not even Sid's "friends" in high places could get them a pass. What could they do?

I began to understand Suzie's situation.

'I see, it must have been very difficult'.

'It was awful. I felt so guilty and so powerless. Guilty at having ignored Ben most of his life and powerless to do anything, helping Edith, going to the funeral, making amends above all.'

And at this Suzie Bell's composure deserted her and she burst into tears. I instinctively put my arm around her and held her for a while. Two women joined in mourning a dead child. This lasted only a short while though, Suzie was too resilient. She dried her eyes, got her compact out, checked her make up and told me the rest of her story.

The situation in Brighton was getting more and more tense and many people wanted to leave the city, but not Edith. With Ben's death she had lost a bit of herself. She spent her days cuddling the boy's dog and hardly responding to the neighbours' offers of food and comfort. She had become a recluse and wouldn't leave the house that was so full of Ben's memories. Even going to the shelter was too much for her. Suzie had tried to help Edith but Sid was not prepared to lose everything he had invested in her career and when the studios in Brighton closed, he dragged her to London. Suzie was not to see Edith ever again, as the poor woman followed her little son and was killed in what became the 'Brighton Blitz'.

'I didn't have any reason to go back to Brighton, no family, nothing. London offered me a future, with or without Sid.'

'Why, what happened to him?'

'I caught the eye of a producer and got my first big break. Sid didn't want to let go of me and got nasty but by then I had a new protector.'

'And there is where your career really took off,' I commented.

'Yes, and do you know what? It was then that I really grieved for my little brother. The tears I shed in the dramatic scenes were more than playacting, I could see his story reflected in the wartime movies and him as another victim of the war.'

There was nothing more to say. We now understood one another. The only thing left to do was to walk towards the cemetery where Ben's new headstone stood out against the darkening sky.

Somebody was walking behind us and I turned towards him. I looked into the same handsome face, blue eyes and winning smile as all those years ago and then looked at the boy standing at his side. Remy, my husband, pushed him towards us 'Go to your mother, Ben.'

Ends.

Printed in Great Britain
by Amazon